Beautiful Mess

Heather Finch

Contents

Chapter One

M aroon 5   Cold

*****

The sound of my phone ringing sends my eyes open.

Are they serious? Like is this person serious?

I lean over the nightstand to check the display and I raise a brow.

I don't bother answering as I mute the phone.

I fall back on the bed and the warm body pressed to mine registers.

What the hell?

I sit up again to access how much of a bother this warm body will be, i almost sigh in pain.

Swear to God Marcel can be a fool sometimes, he's my brother but a fool nonetheless.

The person beside me moans in her sleep and I almost feel bad about waking her.

Almost.

I don't feel bad about anything, at all.

I stand up, they've succeeded in ruining my sleep.There will be hell to pay.

I turn when the door to my room opens.

"You didn't answer your call"

Marcel says by a way of greeting, he knows very well not to call me on my personal phone.

Infact not to call me at all for no reason.

I decide to let that go, it's isn't worth it, yet.

"I saw no reason to"

I say, replying to his question.

He sighs and glances at the bed.

"Get rid of that "

I say to him as I pad to my bathroom, I do my business and exit.

I see Marcel getting rid of the girl by pressing some cash into her palm and what I am sure is his cell phone number.

"Call me"

He tells her.

She nods and winks flirtatiously at him.I show no signs of emotion when he turns to me.

He winces when he sees my expression.

"When did you sneak her into my room?"

I ask as I move towards the window and he follows.

"Gage....."

"Marcel, I made i clear i wanted a full night sleep, you disobeyed my others..."

"Gage, chill, I just thought you needed to unwind, that's why I sent her up, it's been so long since you had a ...."

I raise a finger and he stops speaking.

His first mistake was using my name, his second was interrupting me while I was still speaking and his last will be to continue speaking when I clearly want him to shut the hell up.

"Get Will"

I say, referring to my second in command after Marcel.

"Why?"

He asks petulantly.

I freeze as I turn to him from my window.

"Did you just question my order?"

I ask coldly and he gulps.

"Boss..."

HE says , going to default mode.

"It's clear you no longer value your life as much as I thought,

It will do you well to remember I can end your life when ever I want to, don't think I can't or I won't.

This...this...thing you have began is getting on my nerves, end it, or I will"

I say to him and he nods.

"Good, now get will, he will be driving me and debriefing me.

You're on probation for the time being"

I say to him and he nods.

"Thank you for your kind consideration, boss"

He says and I don't bother to respond, it's the best I can do for him.

Someone else would be on the floor bleeding from a broken jaw right about now.

I let him get away with much because he is my brother.

And much is little and little is too much.

I notice him move away to do my bidding and my hands go to my head, massaging my temple.

I feel a massive headache coming on, it's a lot of work being strong all the time.

Being Garrett Grayson is hard work, keeping my reputation as strong and as stiff as it is is even harder work.

I didn't build this empire to watch it crumble at my feet because I couldn't separate my personal life from my business life.

Although the means I used in getting to the top is not a very clean one, the end as they say justifies the means.

I am powerful, strong and a f**king force to be reckoned with.

I didn't get there by letting my brother walk all over me.

My Mama might disagree and might be disappointed but that's the way it has to be to keep her in the Channel suits and the red bottomed heels she loves so much.

My doors open and I turn.

"Good morning boss"

"Tell me what I need to know"

"We have received an order to deliver a hand made Italian shoe personally to a South African delegate that just arrived at the African National Conference in Ghana"

He says, going directly to business.

"What's the duration on this delivery?"

"Two days boss"

He says and I nod.

"Any words for the recipient from our sender?"

"No sir"

I nod and he exits, knowing he has being dismissed.

I turn back to the window.

I haven't had a full night rest in a week and yet I still have more job to do.

In my line of work there is no resting, when you snooze you get killed.

You are always on the move and on the lookout for scavengers.

To the world I am Garrett Grayson, importer of hand made Italian shoes and bags.

That's just a front for what I really am.

It's makes my Mama sleep better at night .

In reality, I am a highly paid assassin and mercenary for hire.

I am a criminal and I will have it no other way.

I speak into my phone."Get the plane ready boys, we are going to Ghana"

"Yes boss"

This operation should be a piece of cake, in and out, just as I like it.

In and out.

AN.

Heya, Bebe here.

Please enjoy this novel, thank you, it's going to be the best yet.

Gracias!

At the beginning I have added a song I listened to while writing, it's something I do.

I have a playlist for writing, I know,am weird.

Lol.

If you loved what you just read, consider giving it a vote and commenting.

Thanks!

Chapter Two

Ariana Grande   Into You

Kismet.

"Calm down Mimi, you are making me nervous"

I say to my best friend as I listen to her pace around.

I feel her stop in front of me and I sigh.

Here comes the lecturing, and as always, she doesn't disappoint.

"Calm down? Did you just tell me to calm down? Kismet we missed our flight, we missed our bloody flight!"

"Am aware"

I say as calm as can be, that seems to set her off.

"You can't be calm about this!!, We might miss your surgery!"

"Am aware"

I repeat.

"Kismet..."

She begins to growl and I hold up a hand, she stops.

"Mimi, I have been living with this condition for 20 years, am sure a one day delay on my surgery won't kill me"

I say, trying to reason with her, but alas, she doesn't want to be reasoned with.

"Your father will kill me if I don't get you to Ghana, Kis, he will kill me, Me!."

And for what? Just because I couldn't say no to that asshole Kevin."

She says.

Oh, wait.

Did I forget to mention this is her fault?

That she totally forgot our scheduled time because she was having a raunchy night with her friend that she refuses to call a boyfriend?

"The situation will solve itself, just watch"

I say to her and she stops pacing the sitting area of the airport to take a deep breath.

"You are right, I have to fix this, shouting won't help"

I nod my head solemnly.

"You know what, am going to go see if there is someone I can talk to that will help me sort through this mess"

She says.

"I hope you will be okay alone"

"Am not a child Miranda, go"

"Stay here Kis, I will be back soon"

I almost roll my eyes, I would have if I thought she would see it behind the giant sunglasses I am wearing.

I feel her step away and I seat in silence, my hand going to the necklace on my neck.

I trace the heart shaped necklace with my hand as I wait.

It's one of the only thing I have of my mom's, after she died, my Papa made it a mission to get rid of everything that reminded him of my Mama.

I held on to the necklace.

I sigh as I wait.

I feel this is going to be a very long wait.

Mimi is everything but a diplomat .

I settle back on my seat.

∘∘∘∘∘∘∘∘∘Garrett.

"What do you mean we have to wait for the plane to refuel?"

I growl at Will and Marcel.

They take a step back.

"Boss..."

"I work with a bunch of idiots..."

I say out loud while scrubbing a hand down my face.

I look around the waiting area to see it deserted, it's almost empty except for a girl sitting a little ways away.

It's a small airport for local flights, so it's expected.

What I did not expect was for my boys to tell me I have to wait.

"How long?"

I growl out.

"30 mins boss, an hour tops"Marcel says and I feel my jaw pop.

A whole hour.

I give a sharp nod before I move to take my seat.

When we get back from Ghana, I am going to make it a priority to teach these two bozos what they seem to have forgotten.

I take a seat near the girl who seem to have dosed off and I wait.

I stay like that for about 5 minutes, checking some updates on my phone before the silence is broken by a...

"Hi"

I pause.

I take a look around.

Is she talking to me?

"You are not sleeping are you?"

She asks.

And yes, she seems to be talking to me.

"No"

"Okay, good"

She says before going silent again, I wait for her to continue but she doesn't, after a while I go back to my phone .

"Where are you going to?"She asks.

"Ghana"

I reply shortly, am sure my tone has made it clear that I am not in the mood for any form of conversation.

It's either she doesn't hear it or she choose to ignore it.

"So, Ghana, that's great, am going there too."

She says and I nod, going back to my phone for the millionth time.

"Business or pleasure?"

She asks.

"What?"

"Are you going for business or pleasure?"She asks again and I give up on trying to use my phone.

"A little of both"

I say to her and she nods, I turn my full attention to her and wait.

Even grown ass men find it hard to meet my gaze head on.

She doesn't flinch but instead continues, I raise a brow.

"So what's keeping you?"

She asks.

"Am waiting for my plane to refuel"

I say to her and her breath catches.

"You have a plane?"

She asks and I almost roll my eyes, typical women.

I could almost see the dollar signs on her big ass sunglasses.

I don't bother to respond but instead ask a question of my own.

"What's keeping you?"

"Oh, I and my friend missed our flight, she was having a crisis so we forgot"

I nod.

She doesn't seem to be bothered about missing her flight.

"You must be angry at your friend then"

I say.

"Why should I be?it could have happened to any one"

She says and I feel my brows raised.

The baffling thing is that she said that with all sincerity and no pretense.

I feel my interest peaked.

I might have made a mistake on my earlier assessment.

"So where's your friend?"

I ask, finally.

"She went to see if there is anything she can do".

"So, you are here alone?".I ask.I don't know why I am initiating conversation with this girl but I am.

"I don't think I should answer that, you might be a serial killer"

She says and I feel my lips tilt, I chuckle softly and I freeze.

When was the last time I laughed?

I see Marcel and Will look towards this way .

"Am not a serial killer darling, close but still too far, I believe they are classless"

I say and she laughs softly.

It's sounds like bells tinkling.

"You are funny"

She says and I feel something in my stomach, I push it down .

"So, can we come with you on your plane?, We have our passports"

She asks and I don't know when I say yes.

I see Marcel stand straighter at my answer.

"Thank you very much, am Kismet by the way"

She say, stretching her hand forward.

I grab the soft hand before answering.

"Am Garrett"

It takes me a while to realize that I gave her my real name, my name not my nickname.

"Hi, Garrett"

She says and I realize something else.

It's totally worth it to hear her say my name with her bells voice.

Chapter Three

J on Bellion   Dead man walking

Garrett.

I watch her tell her friend about us and I see her friend throw us a suspicious look.

"Are you sure about this Kis?"

Her friend asks, they are not doing a very good job of whispering.

"Am very sure Mimi, he's my friend"

I feel my eyebrows raise and I hear Marcel conceal a chuckle with a cough, her friend's head flies up and I keep my gaze steady on her.

She sighs.

"It's not as if we have much of choice anyway"

Kismet says when she notices her friend giving.

"If they kill us I will come back to haunt you for the rest of your days"

Her friend says.

"If they kill us, I will be dead too, so you can't haunt me,.we will do the haunting together"

Kismet says, a laugh in her voice.

Her friend turns to me.

"Hi, am Miranda"

"Gage"

"Ok, Gage, I just called some of our friends and they know we are getting on a plane with you, so no funny business"

She says and I don't respond, I just keep my gaze steady on her.

If she decides not to come with I won't care.

I don't give a damn either way.

"Boss, the plane is ready".

I rise to my feet and I feel the boys following.

I don't turn to look if the women are with us, I have broken most of my rules today, I won't be breaking anymore.

I get on the little plane and I settle in a seat, pain lances through my head and I clench my teeth.

Damn migraine.

I rest my head back and close my eyes.I can't have this pesky pain disturbing me.

I signal to Will and Marcel with my eyes close.

They know I am not to be disturbed, they know I constantly get this chronic migraines and how I feel about it.

I can get easily irritated.

To put it mildly.

I hear the girls get on the plane with their many luggage, I don't bother asking the boys to help them.

Another rule I won't break.

I feel the pain in my head increase and I clench my fists.

Damn.

I can't have this, seriously.

I feel a warm body settle besides me and my eyes comes open.

They land on Miranda's.

She startles.

"She insisted on sitting besides you"

She says and my eyes go to Kismet's.

She is still wearing her sunglasses.

I see Will step forward.

"Ma'am, am sorry, you can't seat here"

He says.

"It's fine William"

I say and I feel my voice crack.

Will steps away and Miranda does also.

The voice of the captain blasts from the speaker.

I fasten my seatbelt and I rest back.

I feel a touch on my arm and my eyes goes open.

"Can you do mine?"

She says.

"What?"

"My seatbelt"

I don't even bother asking why, I just sit forward and fasten hers.

The plane gets into motion and again i feel a hand on my arm.

"Can I hold your hand? Please? Am not a fan of flying"

She says and before I can answer I feel her feel her way to my hand before slipping hers in.

She clenches my hand and I know if I can see her eyes, they will be clenched also.

I don't know why I did it but I rest my other hand on top of hers and I feel her settle a little.

I feel my headache go down a bit so I rest back.

By the time the plane got in the air my headache had dimmed to a bearable extent.

Even after that I still don't slip my hand out of hers, she doesn't seem to be bothered by it too.

She rests back.

"Thank you"She whispers.

"Yah"

I say and I close my eyes.

After a while she speaks.

"Does it hurt alot?"

"What?"

"Your head, does it hurt a lot?""How did you know?"

"You are clenching my hand"

I go to let her go but she holds tight.

"It's fine, it's okay"

She says and I settle back.

"It's must really bother you"

"I will be fine"

I say.

"You don't have to be strong or act it to me, it's fine to tell me how you feel"

I feel my heart skip a beat.

Who is this girl?

She begins to stroke my wrist and I turn to watch her profile.

"You must be someone important"

She says after a while.

"What gave it away?"

I ask and she laughs a little.

"Your big plane and bodyguards"

She says .

"I thought i was being cautious".

She laughs again.

I see her friend turn to look at us from her seat.

"Miranda's looking this way right?"

"Can't you see her?"

"Haven't you noticed I am blind?"

I go quiet as I watch her.

Now that she mentioned it I notice the way she seems to tilt her ear to every sound.

"Am sor...."

I begin to apologise but I stop.

When was the last time I did so?

"It's fine, am going to be fine soon"

"What do you mean?"

"Papa has found a doctor who believes he can help me regain 90 percent of my sight"

I nod before realizing she can't see me.

"The doctor is in Ghana?"

"Yup, am half Ghanaian"

She says airily .

I feel pain lance through my head again and I instinctively clench her hand.

I close my eyes and I hold my breath when I feel a hand on my face.

She seems to be tracing my face.

"Does it hurt here?"

She asks, her fingers on my temple.

"Ye.. Yes"

I reply, my voice breaking.

I watch her kiss her other finger before placing it on my head.

"It's fine now, you only have good energy"

I watch her lips as she speaks and all I wanted to do at that moment was to kiss her.

We stay like that for a while.

Her stroking my head.Me feeling things I am not allowed to, things I won't let my self feel before a big operation.

I should tell her to find another seat but I can't , I am enjoying her comfort too much.

It's been so long I received any form of affection.

"I like you"

She whispers.

I blink at her.

"You have good energy"

She says and I almost scoff at the irony.

I don't have any form of good in me at all, I am a killer.

"Thank you"

"We should meet after I become prettier"

She says and I know my answer means a lot to her.

"Yes, we should"

I say and she smiles a big smile.

I feel my heart clench because I just lied to her, I won't be meeting her.

She's too good, too pure, i won't taint her with my filth.

But she doesn't have to know that.

This world is big, we don't have to meet ever again.

She rests her head on my shoulder and I lean mine back, my hand still in hers.

We stay like that for the rest of the flight.

****

When we get to Ghana it was already morning.

We step out of the plane, my hand in hers.

"Thanks for the ride Gage"

Miranda says and I nod.

I turn to Kismet.

"Here's my number"

She slips a piece of paper in my hand.

"I trust you to call me"

"I will "

She goes on her tippy toes to kiss my cheek and I stand still.

She slips something cold into my hand and my eyes go to it.

"I will be wanting that back when we meet again"

I begin to shake my head.

"You have to take it, she will feel bad if you don't"

Miranda says.

"Thank you, I won't ever take it off"

I say to her.

It's her golden chain.

The one I noticed her tracing most of the flight.

She steps back .

"Untill we meet again Garrett"

"Until we do Kismet"

Miranda leads her away and I watch her go, after she gets into a cab I look at the necklace in my hand.

I walk to the trash bin nearby and I dump it inside.

The necklace and the paper with her number.

I don't have time for emotions.

I have to keep my head straight.

"Let's go"

I say to the boys.

I did the right thing but why do I feel like I just made the biggest mistake of my life?

AN.

Thanks guys, for reading.

Much love.

Chapter Four

H otel TransylvaniaThe zing song

A year later.

Garrett.

"You have to stay under the radar for a while Gage"

Marcel says to me and I nod.

It was a risk even staying in Nigeria, I turn to him and he bows his head to me.

"Thank you for everything Marcel"

I say to him and he nods, I turn to Will.

"Just one year and we are back, you guys think you can survive till then?"

I ask with humour and he smirks.

I shake my head.

What ever made me think they would betray me?.

These guys are my childhood friend and brother, Will is my best friend and it just is a good thing that he works for me and calls me boss.

Although I run a tight ship, I still make them aware that they are a part of a team.

My team.

The Grayson Team.

TGT.

Jesus, I sound like a sappy fool, am sure the bullet wound has set me to my default.

I wince.

The thought of my bullet wound brings back the pain of lead piercing flesh.

My hand goes to my chest.

It has been a hectic year, after the operation in Ghana.

A successful operation I should say, I have had more.

The last one in South Africa was a bust.

It seems as if I was purposefully lured there so I could be killed.

I sustained an injury from a bullet wound after narrowly escaping death.

The authorities were alerted and it was pure luck that Marcel was able to get me through them.

On the brink of death, I didn't know how I got to Nigeria but I owe it to Will and Marcel.

One thing was obvious, I had people after me, my enemies want me gone.

It's up to me to live and kill every last fucking one of them.And make no mistake, I will.

I feel pain go through my head, stupid migraine.

Apparently,

Mom was worried sick when I arrived Nigeria with bullet wounds and now she wants me to take a year off.

She believes I sustained my injuries by being at the wrong place at the wrong time.

I don't bother setting her straight on the facts.

What ever makes her sleep better at night.

Am just happy she isn't on my case to get a wife anymore.

My wound throbs and I feel my hand snake up to the necklace on my neck.

I immediately feel better when my hand comes in contact with it.

I stroke the heart outline and I think back to how I made Will and Marcel go through the airport trash just to get it back.

I just couldn't throw it away, I don't know why but it has kept me company in the coldest of nights and the darkest of days.

I feel my wound throb again and I openly wince.

"You should get that checked out, it looks infected"

Will says and I nod.

"Tomorrow"

I say.

"What's stopping you from going now?"

Marcel asks and my first instinct was to tell him off but I remember that for the next year I won't be much of his boss.

Although he is still under me and still answers to me but he now makes decisions for himself without consulting me.

Well for the next year any way.

"I have a number for a good specialist we can go to, we have to treat this so as to make sure it heals properly"

Marcel says and I nod.

"Let's go"

I say

"Now?"

He asks as if surprised I agreed to go.

"NO time like the present right?"

He chuckles and we step out of the apartment but not before I grab a gun.

Can't go anywhere without my gun.

******

Kismet.

"You should take a break, you are not a nurse yet, you are just volunteering"

I listen to Mimi on the phone as I massage my feet on the roof of my hospital building.

"Mimi, truth be told, I don't think I am cut out for this"

"Aww, my poor baby"

"Am so tired"

I lament

"Welcome to the real world baby girl, it's as hard as nails out here"

"Sob sob"

I say and she laughs.

"You know you don't have to be a nurse, right? You can see now, you can do anything you want"

"I know, that's why I am trying to give back to the society, I feel like I should"

"Baby girl, you've been giving back to the society for close to one year now, you should really start to focus on yourself"

"But..."

"No buts baby, I know you always wanted to be a florist, we will talk about it when I get there ok?"

"Ya, but.."

"How's the new apartment?"

That immediately takes my mind away from my job.

"Oh , it's divine"

"I told you it will be, I choose it for you"

"Yes, yes,we have already established that without you I can't live, no need to rub it in"

"Just thought it will do you good to remember once or twice"

"Yes, but I have to go now, break is over"

"Ok, love, see you this evening"

She disconnects without saying bye and I slip my feet into my clogs as I walk downstairs.

I really like my job, I really do but it's hard work.

I will have to think about opening my own flower shop.

I know it won't bring in much of an income but still I will love it.

And besides, I have my inheritance from my mother.

I don't want to brag but am stinky rich.

I grin at my thoughts.

I collide into someone and i immediately pour out an apology.

"Am sorry"

I say as I lift my head from his chest where I can see some bandages peeking out.

My eyes meets his and it holds.

"So, it was green"

He says .

"What?"

I say and he blinks, seeming to regain himself.

"It's nothing"

"Am sorry again"

"It's fine"

He says as he steps back , my eyes go to the guys behind him and they look to be surprised at something in particular.

The guy in front of me begins to walk past and I walk towards my station.

I can swear I haven't see him before but I feel like I have.

My eyes fly up from the file I am holding when I remember the necklace on his neck.

I drop the folder and I zoom towards the hospital exit.

It can't be.

Can it?

I look around the lobby but there is no sign of him.

The man I collided with.

He was wearing my necklace, well a necklace like mine, I recognized it from the pictures of me I saw after I regained my sight.

I feel disappointment crush at my shoulders.

I don't think I will be getting that kind of luck in seeing him anytime soon

.

Sigh.

Chapter Five

MagicRude

Kismet.

"My poor baby"

Miranda says as she massages my shoulder and I lean my hear forward to take a sip of my beer.

I grimace when the cold bitter liquid spills into my mouth.

"How do you guys stomach this stuff?"I ask her and she takes her seat besides me.

"You are part of us guys now"She says and I roll my eyes, she takes a bite of her suya before turning to me.

"You should go out on a date"She says matter of factedly and I choke on my beer.

"What?"

"I said you should date, you heard me the first time"

"Yeah, I did but am not ready to"

"I know, that's why I want you to experience the real world"

I frown.

"I would appreciate it if you stop talking like that, because I was blind doesn't mean I wasn't experiencing the real world"

I say with a bit of bark to my voice, she just rolls her eyes.

"I never said that.."

"You insinuate it some times"

"No, I don't, what I mean is for you to remember you have your sight now and it's ok to live a little, it's fine to do things normal people do"

I know she is right.

I sigh, gulping down my beer, it's tastes like ash now.

I take a bite of my extra spicy chicken and I drink more beer.

I can't see to stop thinking about Garrett, I know our meeting was brief but it felt like I met my soul mate.

And now it feels like I have lost them.

"You are thinking about him again, aren't you?"

Mimi asks and I nod.

"How did you know?"

"You sighed, and your hand went to your neck, it's your tell"

"I miss my necklace"

"And you miss him too"

I don't respond.

"You should stop doing that, you should stop holding on to him, for goodness sake you guys were only together for a total of about what? 4 hours?"

"I just..."

"You might never see him again, you should face that reality, it's a big world, and even if you do, you might not even have a way of identifying him, although your necklace is rare, what makes you think he kept it?"

She says and I feel tears threaten.

"Oh baby, don't cry"

"I really liked him"

I lament to my friend, she pulls me into a side hug, my head on her chest.

"Am aware Kis"

"We could have googled him but we don't know his surname, you would have helped me find him right?"

"With all my heart Kis"

"I gave him my necklace so that just by chance if we meet I will be able to identify him"

"Am also aware baby girl"

"Why didn't he call me? Am I not pretty?"I ask.

My hand going to my chest, it hurts.

"You are the fairest in the land baby girl"

She says, making a joke and I laugh a little.

I lie on the ground resting my head on her leg and she strokes my head.

"I saw someone with my necklace today"

"Oh really?"

"Yes, he looked so handsome, he was walking with two guys"

I feel her stiffen and I frown.

"Did you speak to him?"

"I didn't get to, he left before I could"

"Am sorry baby girl"

"It probably wasn't him"

I say.

"It probably wasn't"

She says still stroking my head.

I sit up.

"Our children have to get married to each other "

I say out of the blue and she sputters out a laughing.."What?..."

"We have to make our relationship solid by marrying into each other's family"

I say and ok, I might be a little bit drunk.

"What ever you say Kismet."

"Let's Pinky promise on it"

I say, holding out a Pinky finger

"Oh, the great pinky promise"

She says with a smile before pressing hers to mine.

That satisfies me.

"You have to live a long long life so we can match make our kids together, okay?"

She says and I nod, my head on her lap, I am getting sleepy.

"Oh, my sweet girl, you know I love you right?"

She asks.

"I know"

I say sleepily.

"Good, that's why you have to forget all about Gage"

"Never"

I whisper before sleeping off.

I don't see her shake her head in exasperation because I was sleeping.

ooooooooooooo

Kismet.

The door bell ringing wakes me up slowly.

I sit up from the ground and the Afghan on my body slips away.

"It's ok, I will get it, go back to sleep"Mimi says from the kitchen stove, flipping pancakes.

"No it's fine, I can get it"

"You sure? Aren't you hungover?"

She asks.

"Does that explain the pounding in my head? And does it also explain the bitterness in my throat?"

"Oh, my baby is a grown woman"

I poke my tongue out at her.

She laughs.

I scrub my face as I slip my legs into my flip flops as I walk to the door.

Who is that by the way? It's a weekend, can't they sleep in?

Oh lawd.

My head hurts.

I open the door and I come face to face with..

"It's you!"

I exclaim.

"It's really green"

"What?"

"Your eyes, they are really green"

"Why are you surprised?"

"They were covered the last time

"The last time, we've only met once right?..."

I ask my voice breaking.

"Hello, Kismet"

"It's really actually you"

He smiles and I couldn't help but wonder how lucky I am.

oooo

Garrett.

I don't know when I made the decision to actually live a little.

But I did.

I made Will find out everything about Kismet yesterday and he actually told me that she lives across the hallway from me.

I thought about it all night and I want experience what I see others experiencing.

I came as early as I could because I can't help my self.

I actually feel something different for this girl.

"I think I owe you an apology"

I say and the next thing I feel a ball of clothe hit my chest.

I grunt in exertion and a little pain.

What ever made me think I could live away from this girl?

"I waited"

She says.

"Am sorry it took so long"

"Never make me wait again"

"I promise"

I raise my head to see Mimi standing there looking at me coldly.

I don't know how, but she knows.

Am sure about it.

Chapter Six

A dekunle GoldYoyo

Kismet

I watch him sitting at my kitchen table eating pancakes and I can't explain the giddy feeling in my stomach.

Am so happy.

I am surprised that I could feel so much for someone in such a little time, I wasn't always a believer in the insta-love thing.

But I really still can't explain how I feel right now.

He lifts his head to look at me, our eyes holds, I smile, he doesn't.

I don't care, it's obvious he doesn't have much to smile about.

Am going to fix him, make him all mine.

"Do you work at the hospital?"

He asks and I shake my head.

"I just volunteer, I planned on being a nurse"

"Planned?"

"I don't want to any more, it's hard work, and I always feel like crying when i see someone in pain"

I say truthfully.

A shadow passes through his eyes, I don't ask what wrong.

Instead I ask.

"What were you doing at the hospital?"

"I needed an injury to get checked, it seemed infected"

I sit up.

"Is it better now?"

He nods.

He goes back to his breakfast and we stay like that for a while.

I open my mouth to speak but he beats me to it.

"Am sorry I didn't call"

I frown in surprise, one of the things you learn when you are blind is to quickly learn how to read tones, body language and body expressions.

After I got my sight i added reading facial expressions to it.

Humans are so open with their thoughts, i haven't met a person I couldn't read, even just a little.

I haven't met anyone except Garrett.

He's hard to read, his eyes are too cold, his manners too harsh.

He feels to me like someone who prizes self discipline above all things.

When he apologized, I got the feeling that he normally doesn't.

But he did to me, it sends a warm tingle through my system.

I beam and I can see his eyes trace my smile.

My eyes goes to his chest and I beam wider at my necklace there.

"Am happy you kept it"

His eyes follows mine to his chest before lifting to me.

"It was the best present i have ever received, still is"

"It was my mom's"

He pauses for a moment before speaking.

"Am honored"

I smile but lift my head when Mimi enters the room.

She left Garrett and I to have some privacy while she bathes.

"Ohh, looking sharp"

I tease her,

She does a little twirl at the doorway and I laugh.

Her attention goes to Garrett and I don't know why I tense, I get the feeling that Mimi doesn't like Garrett.

But it's stupid, it's not as if they have ever met, except when he took us on his plane.

Wait...

"How come you have a plane and still live in an apartment building?"

I ask out of the blue and I almost slap my mouth, stupid me, always saying the first thing that pops into my head.

He grimaces, as if uncomfortable.

"You don't have to answer that"

I say quickly.

"No, I would like to hear his explanation, or wait, did you lie to us?or did you go bankrupt?"

Mimi asks and I shoot her a look .

Cool it down girl, I have been waiting for this man all my life.

"You are right, the company I work for went bankrupt, I had to move out of my town house"

He says and I feel my hear clench.

"Am so sorry about that, it must have been painful to leave a place where you feel secure"

I say and he nods, Mimi snorts.

I throw her another look.

What's up with her?

"Kismet, I left my red bag in your room, please help me get it, some files I need for work are inside"

Mimi says and I nod.

"Ok, get some breakfast, I will be back"

I move to my room, I hate to leave her with Garrett but i also have to get her bag.

Mimi's boss is a hard man to please, she works as his Personal Assistant.

I exit the room.

******

Garrett.

Lying has always come easy to me, it's one of the things you have to learn when you work the kind of job I do.

In all my life i have never regretted lying as much as I did today.

It was so easy to tell her that I was bankrupt while in essence i am as rich as the president of my country.

When she gave me her sympathy, i felt like the scum of the earth, no, I felt lower than that.

"You have to go, you have to stay away from her"

I turn to Mimi.

I won't insult her by acting oblivious to her concerns.

"How did you know?"

I ask.

"After the surgery, she almost killed herself waiting for you to call, i had to do something, I investigated you, I didn't find anything good"

"Did you tell her?"

"What do you think?, You think she will be smiling at you the way she is if she knows? You think she will be head over heels in love with you if she finds out you kill for a living?"

I don't respond.

"It must have been pretty darn good"

"What?"

"The resources you used in investigating me, it must have been pretty darn expensive"

"That's not what I ..."

"Mimi, let's not do this, you know my reputation, you know when I want something I go out of my way to have it.

I want your friend, for the life of me I dont know why, I just know that I want to make her happy.

You can't get in the way of that, I will misplace you"

"Grayson...."

"How do you think she will feel knowing the only family she has after her father works for the NSS? {National Security Service} that you constantly put your self in danger?

That one day you might go to work and not come back? That you don't actually work for a PR firm as you make her believe?"

"Are you blackmailing me?"

"Yes"

I state.

When I asked Will to get me Intel on Kismet, he got some on Miranda too, knowing I will be interested to know that Miranda works for the country's secret service.

These people have been out to get me.

She chuckles dryly.

"You should be glad am not sending you in"

"You should be glad am not taking the gun you have in your waist band and shooting you with it"

She sighs.

She speaks after a short pause.

"You can't hurt her"

"I plan not to"

"I will kill you if you do"

I don't respond.

She steps back when we hear Kismet coming into the room .

"This is between us"

She says and I give a sharp nod.

"Am here, you messy human ,what did you do to my room?"

Kismet asks and Mimi kisses her cheek.

"See you later?"

Mimi says.

"You didn't have breakfast"

Kismet notes.

"Am fine, take some drugs for your hang over okay?"

"Yes Mom"

Mimi nods before exiting the room,not even once looking at me.

AN.

Hola

Thanks for reading.

Have a great week.

Chapter Seven

I magine DragonsAmerica

Kismet.

"Are you really sure about this?"

Mimi asks me and I nod, helping her to stir the cupcake mixing.

"You barely know the guy Kismet"

"I can't deny what I am feeling"

I say as I like the batter from my fingers.

"Feeling? Feeling? What exactly are you feeling? Kis, you barely know anything about the real world, you've been single all your life and now you think you are the relationship expert?

Don't you think you should actually look before you leap?"

She says and I stop what I am doing to look at her.

"It's just one date Miranda, it's not as If I told the guy I would be having his babies.."

"You might as well have.."

"What's that supposed to mean?"

"You hold your heart on a sleeve baby girl, you are too kind, it's your type of vibe that make people want you and want to ruin you"

"Ruin me?"

I ask in confusion.

"They are drawn like a moth to flame, you shine and they want to stay under your glow, when that isn't enough they want to steal the light for themselves"

"Miranda, Garrett isn't like that.."

"How do you know?!?!"

"Is there something you know that you aren't telling me?"

"No"

"Then what's all this?"

I ask.

"Am just scared for you"

"Why? You barely know Garrett, don't you think your reaction is a little on the extreme?"

That seems to get to her and she takes a deep breath before setting down the ladle.

"What am just saying is that if in any way you feel indebted to him, you shouldn't, we can even pay him for the ride on his plane.

You don't have to date him, we can start your dating life with someone else, someone secure"

She says, pleadingly

"But that will be boring"

I reply truthfully.

"Oh, wait, I get it, is this a bid to satisfy your insatiable taste for adventure? Do you think your life is a game?"

"Mimi. . . ."

"You are acting like a child Kismet"

"For the love of God Miranda!!"

I shout and that seems to shut her up.

She blinks at me, I never get angry but right now am pretty pissed.

"I am not a child you should coddle Miranda, and also you are not my mother, I love you and everything but what I need now is a friend not a mother.

If or when I make a mistake, it will be mine to make, if ever I get my heart broken, I would expect you to be there with lots of chocolates and ice cream.

Please don't kill what ever I have now just because you have some misgivings about the guy and you don't want to tell me.

Only heaven knows why that is! "

I take a deep breath and I watch her consciously make an attempt to drop the topic.

I smile.

Mimi is a control freak but she is still my friend and I love how protective she can be sometimes.

She's like an open book most times and other times like a sealed vault.

I won't have it any other way.

"Ok, do your thing, i will be here waiting for you "

She says and I pull her into a hug.

"I would appreciate if you don't insinuate that the relationship I am starting will end soon"

I say before pinching her butt.

"Ouch that hurts".

"You deserve it for making me shout"

"I just..."

"It's fine sweetie, it okay"

"I love you too and everything"

"What?"

"You said you loved me and everything, am just replying"

I shake my head.

She's so cute.

******

"Are you sure about it?"

I ask Mimi later in the night when we have gorged ourselves on cupcake and milk.

"Yes,it's in one week"

I sigh.

Although I was blind due to abnormal birth defect that was rare but thankfully treatable, I had to get surgery.

And now I have to constantly go for check-up out of the city every other month.

It's not as If I can see clearly but with the aid of glasses and contacts I manage.

But straining my eyes to see far is a big no no.

"What's wrong?"

Mimi asks when I sigh again.

"I had thought Garrett will ask me out on a date next week"

She chuckles before replying.

"What's stopping him from asking you out this week and also what's stopping you from asking him out your self?"

"Can I ?"

I sit up eagerly before slumping back down again.

"I can't , am too scared"

"All the girls do it nowadays"

"Have you?"

"Well no.."

"See".

"It's just because I don't have time for dating now after Kevin"

"That's a lie, you have a crush on your boss"

Her mouth hangs open and I smirk.

"What kind of absurd statement is that?"

"It's so obvious"

"Kismet..did you go through my bag?"

"I didn't but it's really so obvious, when you talk about him you get them dreamy eyes and you twist your hair around your finger and you sigh like a love sick bird"

"I don't !"

She exclaims

"Keep kidding your self, you are pretty easy to read"

She rolls her eyes.

"It can't happen between I and my boss, he's too macho and you know how much I like my control"

She says looking everywhere but at me, I frown before realizing.

"Miranda! , Did you sleep with your boss?"

"No! "

"Mimi..?"

"Ok, fine, we kissed and after that he wanted me to move into his house, ha! As if!"

I roll my eyes.

"You have pretty much moved into mine"She throws a pillow at me and I dodged, poking my tongue out at her.

"You know how much I love my little cottage"."Am aware, you even named it"

I say.

"See? It can't work between us"

"I don't see, the only thing I see is you trying to find every excuse not to be with a guy that clearly likes you enough to want to live in the same house with you"

"When did you get so wise?"

"When you were sleeping"

She laughs and I see that she wants to drop the matter, I do.See?

She's pretty easy to read.

I kiss her head before settling back into her arms.

*****

Garrett

"Boss you might want to see this"

I raise my head from the file am reading when I see Mimi standing at the doorway.

I stand and walk to her.

"What?"

"I want you to ask her out on a date this week"

"Excuse me?"

"She wants you to ask her out, make it this week"

"I planned on doing just that"

"Good, don't take her to anywhere fancy, she doesn't like it"

I don't respond and she begins to back away.

I have to set things straight.

"Miranda, let this be the last time you attempt to attach a command to a statement while you are talking to me"

"You can kiss my ass Grayson"

"Not for a million bucks"

"You asshole, don't know what my friend sees in you"

I don't reply and she leaves.

I turn to the boys.

"Find me a restaurant that's not too fancy but at the same time classy, rent the whole thing out for tomorrow evening"

"Yes boss"

Will answers and I go back to work, closing the door.

AN.

Chapter Eight

Vancouver Sleep ClinicSomeone To Stay

Kismet

I am so nervous, really, am really nervous, it's as if he can feel my nervousness or maybe it's just me talking.

He pulls out a chair for me and I take my sit,he does the same thing across me.

"Nice place"

I comment , he nods.

"Why is it so empty?"

He doesn't reply.

"You don't talk much do you?"

He lifts his head and shakes his head at me.

"I thought so"

After a beat I comment.

"You have to talk, it can't be only me doing the talking okay?"

"I will respond when you ask a question"

He says.

"That's not enough"

"It isn't?"

I shake my head.

It's as if he has split personality disorder, when he came to my door earlier this morning to ask me out on a date, he seemed different.

A little nervous even, but right now, he looks in control, as if nothing can get to him.

A though occurs to me that makes my heart clench.

"You don't feel like am forcing you into this right?"

I ask my fear and it won't take the spirit of discernment to hear the worry in my voice.

He pauses before lifting his head.

"I don't do things if I don't want to Kismet, no one can force me into doing anything"

"Am just scared.."

"I am too"

He admits and I melt a little that he can confess his insecurity to me.

"You are?"

He nods.

"Am a bad man, I have done bad things, I don't deserve you, but yet I still find my self clinging to you like a last resort.

I don't want to ruin you Kismet, you are pure,you are perfect, if for any reason I should stand up and exit this room because I don't deserve to sit at the same table with you"

He says finally and I feel tears prick my eyes.

How lonely he must have been to make him think he doesn't deserve to be with me.

"I don't care what you've done"

"You won't be saying that if you actually knew"

He says.

I smile, standing up and going to sit next to him, he tenses, I laugh before saying.

"It's fine Garrett, what ever you've done before me is none of my business, I don't care, I forgive you so you can forgive your self"

He blinks and I see the emotions written on his face.

"You won't be saying that if you kne..."

He begins with a broken whisper and I shush him with a finger to his lip.

"It's none of my business"

I reply with a whisper.

"I don't.. seriously don't care, I have all of you now, I won't let you share you with all of your guilt and demons, you are mine"

He blinks

"Who are you?"

"Am Kismet"

He looks at my eyes for a moment before saying.

"You make me want to be better, you make me want to forget everything i have done, you feel like a clean slate"

"I don't want to be your clean slate, I want to be what keeps you clean Garrett"

"You make me want to be clean"

"Am glad baby"

He kisses my head and I speak in his ear.

"Listen up, you can't feel guilt when you are with me, you have to smile more, you are owned by someone now, okay?"

"Okay"

"Good,then, please, commence with your smile"

"What?"He asks in confusion.

"You have to smile, I want to see you smile"

"I don't smile"

"Everybody smiles"

"I am not everybody"

"I am aware"

He tilts his head to study me.

"You are serious"

HE says.

"Serious as a heart attack, baby"

"Well baby, I won't smile"

I almost smile at him making a joke but I don't, I don't want to draw any attention to him being a little carefree.

"Then baby, I just have to make you"

"I would like to see you try"

HE says.

"Game on, you know you have to smile at how cute I am right?"

He looks unimpressed.

"Is that all you've got?"

He asks.

"Ok, I have to bring out the big guns"

I say wriggling my fingers.

"Don't even think about it"

He say.

"What?"

I ask innocently.

"Don't even try it"

He says, leaning away from me.

I raise my hand and he jumps up , laughing.

"Swear to God, Kismet I will kiss your face off "

He says , laughing.

I stop and i lean back.

"Mission accomplished"

He stops laughing abruptly before taking his sit.

"Is something wrong"

"You are too good to be true"

He says.

"You should know that, you shouldn't ever try to leave me"

"Umm"

"Promise.."

"Kismet. ."I don't say anything more on the subject.

"So could you please proceed to kiss my face off?"

I ask and he smirks.

"That I can do"

He pulls my gently close and he kisses me for a long time.

For a first kiss , it wasn't so bad.

*****

Garrett's bodyguards watched the woman make their boss laugh.

It was something they haven't seen for a long long time.

It felt good to see him enjoying himself after a long time of trying to achieve everything and trying to make everyone happy at his own expense.

They knew this thing wouldn't last long but at least he could enjoy himself for a while.

He was too tainted to really live a normal life.

They all understood that.

They look away when he kisses the woman passionately, it was too beautiful for words.

They could feel their respect for the woman growing, that she could give of her self without wanting more back.

This were the thoughts running through their mind.

Well at least one of them, the other one was just plain bored and scheming.

Thinking malicious thoughts on how to use the girl in hurting the man.

He clenches his fist.

He must see to the end of this man, the man who thinks he owns the world.

Chapter Nine

B ob MarleyRedemption song

Kismet.

"So how is it?"

I ask Garrett from over across the kitchen counter.

"It's taste like solid acid"

He says truthfully, i pout, he seems to reconsider his answer.

"It's tastes great, really awesome"

He says and I frown.

"You are such a little liar, I will go with your earlier assessment"I say as I dump the samosas in the sink.

"You should give up trying to cook"

He says, wiping his mouth and hand.

"I think I will"

I say and he pulls me into his lap as I walk towards him.

I twine my hand across his neck and I speak.

"You know, I don't like giving up"

"Am aware"

"You are ?"

"Am here, aren't I?"

I smile and he kisses my head.

"How's your shoulder?"

I ask and he nods.

"It's better"

"Want me to get a look at it?"

I ask and he nods.

"I need some TLC"

He says and I laugh.

"You are gonna get some"I say.I get up to get my first aid kit and I think how awesome the past two weeks have been.

It hasn't been a small feat getting him to loosen up and live a little, he's so stuck in his ways.

We've gone out on a couple of dates, and once to a public place, he wasn't so comfortable there so we left.

I have understood his need not to be in public or were there are lots of people, he doesn't like it.

So I kind of try to make sure we are always indoor.He has start to let me in, he makes jokes now, he laughs and smile.

Although those are rare and far between, I will take them as they come.

If I am told to explain why I feel this way towards him, all I can think about is completion.

He completes me, he feels a need in me I didn't think I had.

I walk back to the sitting room to see him sitting on the floor by the couch, his attention on my ringing phone.

"It's your dad"

He says .I tense.

What does he want ?I walk to the coffee table and I mute my phone, I can call him later, it's not as if he can't wait.

I don't want him to ruin the mood I have going with Garrett right now.

I set the kit down and I kneel besides him, I help him unbutton his shirt.

I swallow at the smooth brown skin beneath the shirt, our eyes meet and o look away.

Am not a fool, although I am completely innocent about what happens between couples, I won't deceive myself to think that the tension between us is nothing but sexual tension.

My hand goes to stroke the skin but he grabs it.

"Please Kismet, don't start, am just a man"He says quietly.

I gulp and nod, we take off his shirt and I lift the bandage.

Again, I am not a fool, my time in the ER has been educating, I know a bullet wound when I see one. I don't ask because I believe he will tell me when he is comfortable enough to do so.

I unwrap the bandage and I dab a little at the red skin with some peroxide.I disinfect and clean.

I begin to reapply the bandage as I say.

"Does it hurt?"

"No?"

"Am sure it's beyond painful"

"You make it better"

He says softly and I slowly raise my head to see him watching me .

I smile and his eyes trace my smile.

"I don't ever want to loose you"

He says out of the blue and I blink, although my heart melts a little because it seems he is starting to like me.

It also clenches because him telling me he doesn't want to loose me means there might be a situation in the future were he has to.

"I don't ever want to loose you too, I promise to wait , no matter how long, I will be waiting"

"Promise?"

He asks.

"I promise, with my heart soul and body"

"I promise to return to you, with my heart soul and body"

I nod, I shift the kit as I kiss his head.

He pulls me close, laying me in the ground, putting weight on his injured shoulder and chest.

"Garr, your shoulder"

I say, he doesn't say anything, he just leans down and kisses me full on the lips.

I begin to protest because of his shoulder but he tangles his hands in my hair and pulls me closer.

Soon, I forget all about his chest and concentrate on how his kisses are making me feel.

He begins to trail kisses from my face to my neck and I close my eyes, is this...?

"Sorry for interrupting"

A very bored and unapologetic voice says and my eyes fly open, Garrett slowly sits up, kissing me softly on my lips one last time.

I must not have heard the door open because Miranda is standing there glaring at us like she is my mother and she caught me with a guy .

"How long have you been standing there"

I ask her, she doesn't reply, her eyes on Garrett, glaring at him.

"Mimi, when did you arrive?"

I ask her, putting all emphasis on my tone, silently asking her not to make a big deal of this.

I don't know why but Garrett and Miranda hate each other..

I am not exaggerating, they really do, they try to hide it from me but it's hard not to see.

"Miranda James, are you going to glare at my boyfriend all day?"

"We have to talk, tell him to get out"

She says and I am appalled

"Miranda!"

"Tell him to beat it, he has been here long enough"

"What is wrong with you?"

I ask her.

"I don't like your boyfriend, I haven't actually hid it from you have I, he can leave now"

Garrett stand up, pulling on his shirt.

"See you later hazel yeah?"

He asks and not even his nickname for me smooths things over.

Miranda is acting like a little brat.

"No, wait Garrett, I am coming with you, Miranda can stay here alone"

I say to him and I exit the room to get my sweater.

"You aren't seriously going to leave me here and go with him will you?"

She asks me as she follows me to the coat closet.

"Watch me"

"You can't do that, I was your friend first before he became your boyfriend"

She says and I almost laugh.

"Will you just listen to yourself? Is this what this is about? Petty jealousy? About who knew me first? Are you going to ask me to choose next?"

"No but.."

She begins.

"Am going on an evening stroll with my boyfriend Mimi, get used to it, prepare something while you are here and think about how much of a child you are acting like"

I say to her, walking towards the sitting room to see Garrett exiting the door, I run after him and I catch him in the elevator.

I enter with him and I intertwine our hands together, resting my head on his shoulder.

He pulls me close, his hand going around my waist.

I close my eyes and I inhale a deep breath .

This man is my life.

Chapter Ten

D rakeIn My feelings

Kismet.

"Am sorry about Mimi's behavior"

I say to Garrett as we sit on a bench by the sidewalk in the park looking at running children and barking dogs.

"I told you not to apologise again, it's fine"

"Are you sure?, You've been pretty quiet since we got here"

"Am sitting beside the most pretty woman , forgive me if I am quiet and I want to savor the moment"

"You flatter me"

I say with a hand on my chest m, I bat my lashes to make it comical.

He shakes his head as he pulls my head to his shoulder and kisses below my ear.

I shiver a little.

He whispers.

"Cold?"

"Maybe just a little"

"You sure?"

He asks.

I don't reply, he is fishing and I am not below a little childishness.

"I want ice cream"

I say as I see a kid gorging himself on ice cream, it's dripping down his chin and I almost swallow my tongue.

"Okay, let's get you some ice cream before you dive the little kid"

He says and I hit his chest playfully, I poke my tongue at him.

He goes to pull me up but stops, instead saying.

"One day, am going to kiss you so hard and so long I won't come up for air"

He whispers.

"Waiting for that day baby"

He tugs on my hair before stepping away to get me some sweet goodness .

"Newly Weds?"

A voice asks and I turn.

"What?"

I ask a pregnant woman who sets her bag on the ground and sits besides me.

"Your husband looks pretty possessive of you"

"He's n.., we are not..."

"It's fine dear, I have been married for close to 2 years now and it still takes me sometime to wrap my head around the gloriousness I feel when am asked about my husband"

"But he's not..."

"This is my first baby with John, we are hoping it's a girl"

She says talking over me.

"Where is your husband?"

I ask her.

"He's getting me some popcorn, I have a craving"

I nod my head.

"How far along are you?"

I ask , my eyes going to her swollen stomach, she looks so pretty.

"4 months"

She says, rubbing her back.

"Wow, that's big for 4 months"

I exclaim and she laughs.

"It's going to be a healthy baby, a word of advice, enjoy all the time you can get alone with your man now, because am telling you, when the baby comes, you will be too tired to do things"

She says wagging her brows and I laugh .

"Thanks for the advice"

She nods.

"Can I touch it?"

I ask, nodding to her baby bump.

"Oh sure, go on, if you are really lucky she might say hi"

I place my hand on her stomach and I am awed at the peace it brings.

How wonderful to know that a living being is going to be birthed soon.

The baby kicks and I giggle, Maggie does too, I guess am lucky.

"It really is wonderful"

I whisper.

"Maggie, are you distracting people again with the gloriousness of your belly?"

A voice asks playfully and I lift my hand from her stomach, my eyes going to a man standing beside us.

"They love it"

The woman , Maggie says to whom I presume is her husband.

"Your wife is right, I love it, thank you, it was an honor"

"Oh it's fine dear, this is my husband John, am Maggie"

I shake hands with John and he beams down at his wife.

It's hard not to see that they are in love.

A hand wraps around my waist and I lift my head to see Garrett standing besides me with a cone of ice cream.

"You must be her husband, my wife and yours are now besties"

John says, stretching his hand for a hand shake with Garrett, they introduce themselves.

I open my mouth to tell them that we are not married but Garrett beats me to it.

"Thank you, my wife really needs new friends"

My eyes flies to his and he smiles at me before handing me the ice cream cone, it falls because I wasn't paying attention.

I was struck at how handsome he looked when he admitted we were married.

My hand goes to my chest, it hurts, it's craving what it isn't supposed to

His eyes frown but he doesn't loose his smile, he watches me as I do him.

"Whew, I can feel the tension from over here"

Maggie says breaking my concentration on Garrett.

"Am sorry about..."

I begin to apologise to her but she shakes her head.

"No, it's fine, here let's exchange numbers, we should meet up soon"

She says and we do that .

We exchange air kisses and she moves away with her husband.

When they are gone I turn to Garrett.

"Why did you do that?"

I ask.

"Kismet.."

"Are you playing with my feelings?, Do you know how much you saying that meant to me?"

I ask, almost close to tears.

"I meant every word I said, I want to spend the rest of my life with you, nothing is as it is when I am away from you, I need you to stay"

He says and the tears spill over.

He wipes them.

"I think I am in love with you Kismet"

He says and I sob.

"Please, keep me close and love me most Kismet"

He says again and I sob, again.

"You have all of me, all that I am is what you have hazel eyes"

He says and I laugh softly.

He kisses my head and I close my eyes to savor it.

"I will keep you close Garrett, loving you most is not a problem"

He smiles against my head and I almost cry at how this lovely man has let me fix him.

AN.

Whew, indeed.

Thank you Vancouver Sleep Clinic for inspiring this lovely episode!!!

Thanks lovelies, for reading.

Love you guys so much.

Chapter Eleven

Jason MrazHello, You Beautiful Thing

Kismet

I am burning all over, I seriously am incinerating.

"Are you sure?"

He whispers in my ear and I nod.

"I love you"

He says.

"I love you too, just . . . , I haven't. ."

I clear my throat.

"You can tell me Kismet"

"I haven't . . . , I haven't done this before"

I say in a small voice and he tenses.

He rolls off of me and i tense, why did I have to open my big mouth?

"I love your mouth just right, Kismet"

He says and I blink, I think . . .I think I said that out loud.

"You are not angry are you?"

I ask.

"No, never"He says, pulling me and our sheets close.

I rest my head on his chest and he begins to trace lazy circles on my hip, I shiver .

"Am sorry I rushed you"

He says and I sit up.

"You really didn't rush me, I wanted to, more than anything in the world"

I say and he pulls me back down, he kisses my lip when I get close enough.

"You are mine, I have you, I can . . ., We can do this when ever you want, just not now, okay?"

He says.

"Why?"

I ask, insecure.

"Because baby, you deserve a candle lit dinner, a walk on the beach, flowers, dinner amd the works"

He says and I shake my head.

"I don't need those things, I just want you"

I say and he kisses my head.

"I want you now"

I say again and he tenses.

"Kismet.... hazel eyes.."

I straddle him, letting the sheets pool on his chest as I bend my head and kiss him.

He returns it, deeply, far be it for anyone to say he doesn't need me.

He rolls us over, throwing the sheets over his shoulder.

"We might be needing that later"

I say teasingly and he winks.

"Are you sure about this Kismet?"

"Am sure baby"

I say and he kisses me again, he intertwines our fingers and I close my eyes as I feel him kiss my face towards my neck.

He whispers in my ear.

"Am going to have my way with you now and I won't come up for air, be prepared"He says and I feel my toes curl.

*****

Garrett.

"So these things are called eyes?"

She asks and I nod.

"Wow, what a mystery"

She says with a laugh.

"And these are called lips, ears, nose, cheek"

I say pointing to the various parts of her body, she is straddling me and we are playing a game of name the body parts.

She can't seem to get enough, she's laughing like a loon, it's make me feel awesome to think I bring her such Joy.

If someone told me I would be in bed with a woman I call a girlfriend and after having sex we will play a game of name the body parts.

I would have shot him dead and fed his body to the dogs.

"What are these called?"

She points below her neck, grinning mischievously.

"Those are mine"

I say as I roll us over.

I grunt when I feel the stitches on my shoulder pull.

She coos as she kisses it and I watch her hair.

"I was shot"

I say and she freezes.

"I am aware"

She says after a while.

"What happened?"

She asks.

"I told you I was not a good man baby girl"

I say and I expect her to push me away but she pulls me closer.

"Am sorry you have monsters disturbing you my love"

She says and if before there was any doubt how I felt, it just changed.

My heart has been laid on the ground by her feet.

"I love you"

I whisper in her ear.

"I know"

She says and I pull her again closer, she comes willingly.

We stay like that for a while.

"So. . . ,Are you tired?"

She asks and I shake my head, my hand on her hips , drawing circles.

"Okay, since you aren't, do you think we could . . .um m . . . ."

"Kismet, shut up"

I say before pulling her squealing form under me.

*****

Kismet.

We are sitting by the couch in his apartment, wrapped in his sheets.

It's the next morning, we are still too lazy to take our bath, I can't move without him cos if I do I will be taking the sheets with me.

"How do you stomach that shit?"

He asks, nodding at my bowl of ice cream.

"How do you stomach your whiskey's?"

I ask

"Touché"

He says and I nod my head, I refuse to point out that I got my ice cream from his fridge.

He stocked the thing full for me.

I rest back as I take another bite and he eats his bagels, changing the channels.

"Don't watch football, I want telenovelas"

"Baby, you can only watch that stuff when I am not sitting next to you"

He says before kissing my neck.

As sweet as that was, I seriously need to tune in to my favorite telenovela, it's gonna air soon.

"Garrett, baby, I wanna watch"

I say, leaning back against his chest.

"Shit"

He says before tuning in to my favorite telenovela, he even knows the station.

See, he's a big softie under all the hardness.

I lift my spoon to his lips, not even looking at what i am doing, that's how engrossed I am in the movie.

The cool sweetness falls on my shoulder and he licks it off.

He gives me a bite of his bagel and I chew.

"So that's Macarena, the mother of the guy that just kissed the girl"

I say, attempting to explain the movie for him.

He just says.

"Baby, eat your ice cream and watch your movie, don't bother"He says.

"What will you be doing"

He tilts my head to his, finally getting my attention off the TV,he kisses my lips before saying.

"I will be watching you"

My toes curl and I settle into him as I watch my movie.

Chapter Twelve

L il Dicky Freaky Friday

　　Kismet.

I enter my apartment later in the evening to notice my kitchen light off and a shadow sitting at the kitchen table.

I scream before hitting a light."Jeez Mimi you scared me"

I say to her and she lifts her glass of beer towards me lazily.

"What are you doing drinking in my kitchen?"I ask her.

"You didn't come home last night"

"I wasn't aware we were keeping tabs on me"I say to her and she flinches, I sigh.

"What's wrong Mimi?"

"Am scared that you are mad at me"

She says in a small voice, I almost roll my eyes, Mimi is like an older sister to me.

Ever since she was brought from the orphanage to our home by my parents,I kind of adopted her as my sister.

She can be insecure and aggressive sometimes but that's just her way of self-preserving.

"Am not angry at you, you don't have to think like that"

I say to her, before taking a sit beside her.

"Am sorry I acted like a bitch, I even made some fried rice to apologise but you didn't come home last night, I wanted to knock but I didn't know if you were ready to face me"

She says, delivering a long epistle.

"You don't have to call yourself a bitch Mimi, I understand that you are protective of me, but you also have to understand that I am a grown woman"

"Am aware"

She says in a bored voice, I roll my eyes."Mimi, you don't have to be scared that you will have to share me with anybody, am all yours, okay?"

"Okay"

"Good,I want some fried rice, will you microwave some for me?"

She nods before moving to do so, I stand and walk to my room wearing a big smile as I remember that I a Garrett made plans to Netflix and chill.

I walk to my bathroom and I bath, I finish and walk out tying a big terry robe.

I walk to the sitting room to see that Mimi has set the table and has a new episode of Into The Badlands going.

It's a movie I fell in love with after I got my sight.

I guess she wants to bond too,I miss her.

I sit beside and she comes closer dropping her head on my shoulder.

"You smell nice"She says.

"I always smell nice".

I reply and she pokes me in the side and I laugh, she hands me a plate of rice and I commence the eating and watching thing.

When am done,she takes the plate and sets it on the table, I begin to take a sip of water when she comments.

"So, do you want to tell me how you got the big hickey on your shoulders and neck and almost on your face?"

I choke on my water and she pounds my back lightly.

"What?"

I ask, acting oblivious to her question, she is unimpressed by my act.

"I know you heard me"

She says .

I don't reply.

"Oh my gawd!!!, You totally did it!!"

I hide my face in my palm.

"Oh God "

I lament.

"Oh Jesus, you totally had sex, that's a big ass love bite"

She say, pulling the robe off my shoulder, examining them, I beat her hands off .

"What happened to waiting for the one?"

She asks and I blink.

"Garrett is the one"

I reply.

"You are serious"

She says soberly as if just realizing that I wasn't joking all those million times I told her I liked Garrett.

I nod anyway.

"You really like this guy"She says and I nod again.

"Wow" She says and i nod, yet again.

"Am sorry i made it hard for you,Kiki"She says and I don't respond.

"It means I have to be very nice to him then, seems I will be seeing him for a while"

She says and I beam my approval.

"I love you Mimi"

I say and she laughs before asking.

"So, how was it?" She asks and I blush.

"it was fine.." I say, blushing like mad. "Ehhi, just fine?"

She asks dubiously and I nod, by the way, what does she want to hear.

MY door opens and my eyes go to the shadow at the doorway.

I remember giving Garrett the pass code to my apartment, I didn't know he was going to show up unannounced.

Am not even dressed!

His eyes take in the scene before coming to me.

"I can come back later"

He says and my face falls.

He must have said that because of Mimi.

"it's fine, you can stay, we were watching a movie anyway, wanna join us?"

I turn my head slowly to Mimi like a zombie on drugs, my eyes flit to her expression and I see her clenching her teeth.

Aww, my baby is doing everything to make me as happy as possible, even though she hates my boyfriend's guts.

"Thank you darling"

I say to her before giving her a side hug.

Garrett sits on the highback chair and I immediately move to him.

He cuddles me close.

"I missed you"

He says in my ear and I smile. "We were only apart for 2 hours"

"Two hours too long hazel eyes" He says and I laugh.

"Am right here now, not going anywhere"

I say to and he pulls me close, his hand wrapping around my wrist and I settle into him.

I lift my eyes much later to see Mimi looking at us, when our eyes meet she looks away but looks back at me with a small smile.

I smile back.

Yep, everything is going to be fine.

AN

Howdy my good people

And also on a side note, I need different type of Ghanaian dishes and If possible, links on how to prepare them.

All my Ghanaian readers, fighting!

Chapter Thirteen

I magine dragonsDarkness

Garrett

"What are you doing?"

I ask Kismet when I see her dragging a big box towards my apartment.

She squeals and turns around.

"I thought you said you were not going to be back for another 4 hours."

"I changed my mind, I missed you too much"

I say and right in front of me I see her face melt. My sweet girl.

"So do you want to tell why you are dragging a box as big as you to my apartment?"

She sighs before leaning against the said box.

"It was supposed to be a surprise" She says, clearly put out.

I don't even blink at her statement, we've been together for 4 months now and am used to the fact that my girlfriend believes in surprises.

As much as I hate the concept I have grown used to it.

"So, what's this surprise for?"

I ask and she looks at me like I am crazy for asking that question. I just pick the box from the ground and move it to my apartment, she follows me.

"What's inside?"

I ask.

I don't wait for her reply I just use my car key to open the box and behold there is..

Wait.

"Christmas decorations?"

I ask her and she nods.

"Baby, Christmas isn't for another five days, why do you have to do this now and in my apartment of all places?"

She pouts and I feel my self bracing up for the inevitable fake tears.

I am not disappointed.

"I thought you loved me?"

She asks and I nod. "I don't see how that figures to the Christmas decorations, babe"

"I wanted to do something special for Christmas, I mean, it's our first Christmas together as a couple"

She says and I think I begin to get it.

"Babe..."

"It's fine if you don't like it" She says and I feel like shit

"Go on and do what you want with the house baby girl, it's yours too"

She throws me a big smile and I feel like the luckiest asshole alive.

"So are you going to help me?"

She asks and I begin to shake my head.

"I promise to repay the help with something of my own"

She says and I have a good idea what my payment will be.

"Well, since you asked so nicely"She laughs as I flick her nose.

4 days later.Christmas Eve.

Garrett.****The buffon laughs at my girl like his life depends on it.

What an idiot."If you glare at him any harder there won't be anymore of him to glare at"

Mimi says besides me and I turn to her.

"Are we friends now?"I ask with my drink going to my lips.

"It's Christmas, even you deserve a break"She says and I don't respond.

It's obvious it kills her to see me so close to her friend but it okay if she dies, I don't care.

I will take care of Kismet through the grief.

"Are you plotting my death in your head?"She asks and I almost choke on my drink."What?"

I sputter and she laughs."I knew it, your poker face is loosing it's touch"

I turn to looks at her and for.onxe I don't see my arch nemesis , I just see a girl.

I chuckle and she laughs, I turn to see Kismet smiling at me.

Apparently she is happy I and her friend are getting along.

I beckon her and she falls on my lap, I throw a smug look at Marcel and he looks surprised.

I can't believe I was jealous at my brother.

"Why did you that?"She ask and I turn to her."Do what?"

"You just threatened Marcel with your eyes"

I kiss her neck.

"Are you enjoying yourself?"I ask her and she nods.

"Thank you for inviting Marcel and Will"I say to her.

"They are your family, so..."She says and it reminds me of something.

"Why aren't you with your father on Christmas?"

I ask her and she stiffens.

She never talks about him and I wonder why.

"We are not on good terms, we made a deal not to reach out to each other on Christmas, it's a celebration we don't want to ruin for each other"

"Why?"

"We always get on each others nerves, ever since mom died, he has been different, very different,he's been too protective and judgemental"

I nod.

"I can see my mother being like that "

I say and turns to look at me.

"Is she not a good mother to you?"

"Most times, when it comes to asking things of me"

I say, and she kisses my head."It's a good thing we found each other then"

She says and I nod.

"Do you want to dance?"I ask her when a slow song comes on and she nods.

I stand and pull her close as we begin to dance and she wraps her hand around my middle.

"I love you"

She says to my chest and I pull her closer .

I am so content right now.

Nothing can go wrong.

***

The person looks at them as they dance and he feels so much rage at how happy he looks.It's not fair, it's not fair!He is going to ruin them and kill them and make sure the man regrets everything he ever lived for.

Chapter Fourteen

T he VampsAll Night

5 months later.Almost 1 year.

Garrett.

I feel a hand stroking my chest and I pull the body close.

"When did you wake up?"I ask her and she moans into my chest .

"I didn't get any sleep"She says and I roll over to give her a critical look.

"Why?, I noticed you've not been getting any sleep for sometime now""You always notice everything"She says and I just raise a brow.

She sighs.

"I wanted to watch you sleep" I don't call her out in her lie, I just kiss her lip.

"Eww, you kissed my morning breath" She says and i kiss her again before saying.

"You will tell me if something is wrong right?" She seems to get that I am serious because she nods.

"I will be going out today, let's have dinner when I return, I will pick you up at the flower shop, okay?"

"Ok," I kiss her head and she closes her eyes before whispering.

"I have something to tell you when you return" She says and I nod.

I think I have a very good idea of what she is going to tell me.

I think she wants me to meet her father, am prepared.

You know how they say people don't really change? Well that's a load of bull.

I have been changed by Kismet James.

When I got the call this morning that I am free to go back to my normal routine and that the security agencies are not our for me again and that I even have a client, the first thought that entered my mind was Kismet.

I am going to go out today and keep my reputation and my self clean. I am going to kill Gage Grayson and birth Garrett Grayson.

Am going to be a better man for Kismet.

I turn to her and say.

"Am going to spend the rest of my life with you hazel eyes"

She smiles before snuggling close.

*****"What in hell are you talking about?"

I ask William who seems to be acting neutral to what might soon be the day of his death.

"Sir, we got you out of South Africa with the help of the Shawn's, they are requesting a payment to the debt"

"Why wasn't I ever notified of this problem?"

I ask him, going directly into Gage mood.

"Am sorry boss, but I was in charge of transportation, Marcel was in charge of everything about moving you"

I stiffen.

"Let me get this straight, you know nothing about how I was moved? What do I pay you for"

"I am sorry boss but Marcel told me that he was given orders from you, that I could in no way get involved"

"Marcel?"

Why am I hearing that name a lot?

"Yes boss, I am..."

"Finish that statement and you will be on a liquid diet for all of your life"

He takes a step back.

I close my eyes as I turn away from him.

Apparently, moving me from SA took the power of the South African mob and now I owe them a debt.

They want it in form of me wiping out their rival family.

I drag at my hair, what to do? I know all about debts and payments, in this life you pay up your debts or you go down with them.

I don't have an option and it seems I really don't have any option. My happy ending with Kismet will have to wait.

I can't kill and come back to her. Am going to get this job done and am going to take my girl on an eternal vacation.

I feel a migraine coming on and I scoff at the irony, I haven't had a migraine in almost a year and the moment I step back into this world it comes back.

***

I watch her arrange a bouquet of flower for an old lady while smiling at her and making conversation.

I smile and for once in my life I regret my job, I curse at my father for getting me involved in this shit in the beginning.

And for dying and leaving me without direction.

The woman exits the store and she smiles at me as she does so.

I don't smile back instead I raise my head and I see Kismet smiling and waving at me.

She walks me and we meet half way.

"What's wrong?"

She asks instantly, I shake my head and I hug her close.

"Did your meeting go well?"

She asks but I don't respond.

"Kismet. . . .?"

"Hmm?"

"You know I love you right?"

"I know and I love you too" She says lifting her heads to smile into my face.

"Promise me.. . . ., promise me that no matter what happens you will wait for me. . ."

"Garrett? What's wrong?. . . ."

"Promise me Kismet, promise me that whatever you hear you will always wait for my explanations, promise me."

"Garrett.. .., Am scared"

"Promise me first Kismet"

"I promise"

*****Kismet.

"I promise"

I hear myself saying because it seems to mean a lot to him.

He kisses my head and I rest my head on his shoulder.

We close up and he takes me directly home and directly to his room.

He pulls my bag from me and throws it on the ground,.he begins to pull at my blouse.

"Garrett?"

"Please Kismet, just please, I want to be as close to you as I can"

He seems so vulnerable, I want to ask what's wrong but instead.

I nod and he raises me, my legs immediately goes around his waist.

We kiss to his bed where he proceeded to make me feel as close as I could to him.

Much later when he is sleeping I watch his handsome face.

I finally admit to my self that I am more than scared, I am terrified.

Why did this feel like too much of a good bye?

Chapter Fifteen

K im Min Seung One day

Kismet.

I feel his body rise from the bed and I snuggle deeper into the sheets.

I hear him go through his morning routine, he shaves, brushes his teeth and he bathes.

Still I don't rise from the bed.

When he makes his way to me and kiss my head I finally ask.

"Where are you going this early?"He ceases his kisses to my face to reply.

"I have a meeting today"He says and my heart clenches.

"You will be back right?"I ask and he nods before kissing me again.

"Hurry back, remember I still have something to tell you"

I say and he nods before exiting the room.

I try to go back to sleep but I can't, I lie there worried.

I have no idea why I am though.

I should get up and go to my apartment but I can't.

I want to be around his scent a little more.

I hear the doorbell ring and I finally get up from the bed.

I open the door after wearing one of Garrett's sleeves.

It's Marcel. "Hi, Garrett already left"

I tell him instantly and I almost cringe at how rude I must have sounded.

"Oh" He says his shoulder falling. He must have really wanted to see his brother.

"Do you want to come in for coffee?" I ask him and he perks up.

"Can I?"

"Sure"

I open the door wider and he steps in, we walk to the kitchen and I immediately move to the coffee maker.

As I get the coffee grounds I can't help but notice that he looks nothing like my boyfriend.

Where Garrett is dark and broody, Marcel looks all light and prince charmingish.

I turn to the coffee maker and immediately I get a whiff of the strong smell my stomach roils.

Oh gawd. It's morning sickness.

The doctor said I might get those.

I clap a hand over my mouth as I run to the sink where I dry heave.

"Kismet, are you ok?" I hear him walking towards me so I wave him away.

I pull myself together and I turn to see him standing there looking at me speculatively.

"How far along are you?" He asks suddenly and I blink.

"What?"

I ask.

"For how long have you been pregnant?" He asks again.

"3 months"

"Does Garrett know?"

"No, I plan to tell him this night"

"You Can't" He says and I freeze.

"Excuse me?" "You can't tell Garrett you are pregnant"

He repeats and I scoff.

"Is this a joke?"

"No, it's not, you can't tell Gage, trust me"

I almost tell him to get out and come back when Garrett returns but I find my self asking. . .

"Why?"

"Garrett Grayson is not who you think he is".

"What do you mean?"

"Come with me and I will show you"

He says, I shake my head but he pulls me to a wall, I struggle but he holds tight.

He presses a button and the wall opens. The wall freaking opens.

"What's this?"

I say as my eyes take in the scenes, there were guns everywhere, on every surface.

What is this? Am I dreaming? Am I actually here or am i in a coma somewhere, dying?.

"Do you want to know why you can't tell him? Do you want to know what he does for a living?"

I almost nod my head,I want to know, I really want to know.

"Garrett is..."

He begins but I hold a hand out for him to stop.

"I trust Gage and he will tell me himself"I say as I rush out of the room.

"Are you stupid?"

Marcel yells, he continues.

"Do you think he actually loves you?, You were a fling Kismet,just a distraction, it's time for you to wake up, fucking wake the hell up"

"I don't believe you"I say as I feel my world shattering, my chest hurts.

I clutch at it,it hurts so bad.

"You are so naive Kismet, don't know if you are really innocent or just plain stupid"

He says but I don't answer,i try to concentrate on breathing,on just surviving,on keeping my convictions.

"I will tell you this,if when he arrives today he doesn't offer you an explanation even when you ask, make sure you call me"

He says and I frown,I slowly turn to him to ask .

"Why?""If you know what's good for you, you will call me"

He says before exiting the room.

I slide down to the ground and I clutch at my chest.Why does it hurt so much?

*****Kismet.I hear the door to my apartment open and I tense,he comes into view and I watch him.

I watch him drop his jacket as he walks towards me, I hold up a hand.

He frowns.

"Kismet?"

I take a deep breath and start."I saw your guns today"

He freezes,I literally see all the veins in his body stand out.

"Kismet?"He says again but this time with a little bit of tenderness.

"Please explain Garrett""Just let me hold you in my arms and I will explain, I promise"

I nod and he sweeps me into his arms, he goes to kiss me but I move my face away.

"Kismet please"

"Explain to me Garrett"He shakes his head and I feel my heart break.

"Garrett?"

I ask as a question and he shakes his head again.

I pull away from him standing up and he lets me go."I can't tell you Kismet, there are somethings about me I can't say, not yet, it's to protect you"

"You are hurting me right now Garrett""My love . . . ."

"Tell me please"I say as I feel tears slip down my face.

"Am sorry, Kismet, I. . . . Can't"

I take a deep breath and I almost faint, my hands go to my chest.

I can't believe I have to do this.

"Garrett,...."

I start, taking a trembling breath.

"Do you know why I never called you Gage? Because I knew that's a man with secrets, a man I couldn't handle, a man I wanted but could not have,I came to terms with it, stupid me.

Garrett, I wanted you, I wanted to spend my life with you and am sorry I have to do this but you have to choose, choose between me and your secrets"

He stands, clenching his fist."Don't do this Kismet, please"

"Choose Garrett"I repeat as I feel tears spilling down my cheeks.

"Kismet . . . ""Choose!"I say as I sob.

I watch him and I see him make his decision and it's not the one I wanted.

Not the one I prayed for.

"Am sorry, Kismet"

He says again and I feel pain go through my body with it comes a calming cold.

"You've lost me Garrett"

I say in a cold voice and he stiffens, I see the fear in his eyes but I don't care.

"Kismet, come here"He says but I take a step back.

"You've lost me, Gage"I repeat.

He seems to hate that I called him that because he kicks my coffee table, upsetting the flower vase on top.

It crashes to the ground and it breaks, water spilling everywhere.

It soaks into the rug but I don't take my eyes off Garrett's face.

"Kismet, hazel eyes. . ."

"Get out and never come back"I say to him .

"Kismet. . ."

"Leave, get out"

I say to him and he takes a deep breath.

"I will be back, you just need some rest, we will talk about this tomorrow, I love you.

You can't leave me, we will talk tomorrow"

He says and he waits for me to say something but I don't, he waits some more but leaves after a while.

When the door closes I slide to the ground and sob my heart out.

Oh God.

It hurts.

****

Garrett.

As soon as I clear the doorway to my apartment I begin to let the rage in me pour out.

"FUCK!!!!"

I kick at the door and the wall and any surface I get to.

"Shit"Kismet can't leave me, she just fucking can't.

Am going to kill anybody that stands in the way.

I walk to my room to take a look at the camera footage.

Am sure there is someone who has to die for spooking Kismet with my secret.

AN.

Thanks for reading!

Chapter Sixteen

J anet JacksonMade for now

3 days later.

Kismet.

I hear him outside my door, asking me to let him in, I cry into my pillow.

I know I said I didn't care about his secrets but now I have not just myself to think about.

I sob harder.

Mimi turns to me.

"Are you sure you don't want to see him?"

I don't respond, just curl up in a ball and continue crying.

****4 days later.

Garrett.

I hear her crying through the door, she changed her pass code, I can't get to her, I feel so helpless.

I slide down the wall to sit on the ground, my back against the door as I speak to her through it.

I know she can hear me. She has to hear me.

****Kismet.

I slide down the wall to sit on the ground, my back to the door as I listen to him through the door.

It's been seven days, seven long days since we broke up.

I feel like dying, death will be the sweetest relief.

I rest my head on the door as I listen to his voice sing a song he always does to me.

It's Beautiful Mess by Jason Mraz, i feel tears begin to spill down cheeks.

I clutch at my chest when it feels like I can't breathe. Why does it have to hurt so much.

When he is done he speaks.

"Kismet, I know you can hear me, please let me in, please, let me in"

He says but I can't speak, my chest hurts too much, I slump to the ground, my breath coming in short bursts.

I feel my sight darkening, I can't breathe. I try to call out to him but I can't.

Oh it hurts.

My hand is on the door, trying to get to him, in anyway but I still can't speak.

My other hand goes to my chest as I quietly sob, please, hear me.

I feel wetness down my thighs and I begin to panic.

Please God, not my baby

I open my mouth and still nothing comes out.

I hear him speak as I die in silence.

"I will be back tomorrow Kismet, make no mistake, I will break down your walls and get you back , I love you"

He says and when I hear him move away I feel helpless, it hurts.

Please make it stop.

That's my last thought before I black out.

*****

5 days Later.

I slowly blink my eyes open,why does everything hurt?

I close my eyes when it gets assaulted by harsh light, I moan a little.

I feel a hand pushing me down and that's when I realize I was trying to get up..

"Shh, calm down, lie back down"

Mimi's voice say to me and I lie back. "What happened? Where am I?"

I ask her as I look around. It seems I am in an hospital.

" You are in a hospital,you passed out"That triggers my memory because I immediately ask.

"How's my baby?"I clutch at her hand , dreading her answer.

I try to sense if my baby is still there but I can't .Is it. . . .?

"Your baby is fine, you are both fine"I almost die in relief.

"Why didn't you tell me?, You knew you were in this condition and that you didn't have only yourself to think about and you were that irresponsible?

You missed meals,you cried yourself to sleep,is Garrett really worth loosing your life and your baby's?"

She ask and I feel properly chastised." Am.. . . . Sorry"

"You don't have to apologise to me Kismet, you made the decision to leave Garrett, then you should make a decision to take care of your health and happiness and your baby"

She says.

Even the mention of his name hurts.I feel my self slipping into that dark place in my head and I make a conscious effort to hold it together.

I have someone else to think about.My hand goes to my chest when I feel that familiar pain .

I can't trust my baby to someone who doesn't trust me enough to share his secrets.

I have to take care of myself. My child needs me.

****Garrett.

It's been two weeks now,two long weeks, she hasn't been home and my plan to give her space has been shot to hell.

I have searched everywhere and still no sign of her.

Where's my hazel eyes?I feel my head pound and I rake my hand through my hair.

"Boss, we have to go now"I hear Marcel say behind me and I feel the venom in my chest threaten to spill out.

It's said that you should keep your friends close and your enemies closer.

That's what I am doing.

Marcel stole from me, he stole my happiness and joy,I will take from him what he doesn't have and when he doesn't expect it.

I want to know what his deal is, yes,he won't know what hit him .

I bend to slide the letter I wrote under Kismet's door.It just says 7 things

'Wherever you hide,I will find you"- Garrett

I hope she gets it and understands that it isn't over between us.

AN.

Hey hey.

Don't be mad at me, you know in every love story there must be a trial and tribulation.

Uh uh, so read and enjoy.It's still a loooong ride away and it's going to be bumpy.

Chapter Seventeen

S uranShining

    Kismet.

3 months later.

"What do you think of this color?"I raise my head from the box I am sorting to glance at Mimi.

"Is that for the wall?"I ask her and she nods. We don't know the gender of the baby yet so we are decorating the room in neutral tones.

"I think that shade of teal is great, would look real okay"

She nods and goes back to what she is doing, I dip my hand into the box and I bring out some letters.

It's from Nigeria, Mimi got them from my old apartment, since I have been living in Ghana she has been a sweetheart.

I begin to sort through them and I find that they are mostly unimportant. I get to the last one and my heart freezes.

It's from Garrett. I open it and his familiar scrawl comes into view.

For the past 3 months I have been doing everything to forget about the father of my child.

I have frozen every emotion in me and it has worked, from time to time I get depressed but I do everything available to make myself get out of the funk.

I have a baby to think about, I won't be a selfish mother, I wont hurt my self or my baby just because I got my heart broken.

But it hurts, it hurts so much. I hear a sob and that's when I realize I actually was crying.

My hand goes to my face and it comes away with tears, my hand creeps to my chest were it hurts the most.

Why am I like this? Why can't I just forget him? What did he do to me?

I sob harder and Miranda turns when she hears.

"Kiki?"

She asks as a question and I sob harder clutching my chest.

It hurts, it hurts a lot.

I feel a hand around me and I turn to sob into Miranda's chest.

I pound on my chest, it feels like my heart is breaking.

"It hurts mi. . mi"

"I know sweetie, I know"

"My he. . . art hur. . . ts" I sob harder as I pound on my chest, I think, I think I am going to die.

"Why do I miss him so much? Why? He left me, I asked for him, you went to him right? He told you he didn't want me"

I ask again for clarification and she nods. After I got back from the hospital I couldn't take anymore of the pain so I asked for him, I told Mimi to get him but she reported that he said he wasn't interested.

I was at Mimi's house, he couldn't be bothered to come see me.

He abandoned me.

I waited but he left me. I sob harder as my chest hurts harder.

Why is everything in shades of pain?

*****

A month later.

"What do you mean you don't know the father is ?!"

I rub at my head as my father dearest shouts at me.

He couldn't be bothered to come see me for close to 4 months now and when he finally does he Judges me.

Typical Papa.

"You are a disgrace, I can't believe I gave birth to you, this excuse of a daughter"

I don't flinch, am too used to the way he talks, even the child he is proud of is scared of him.

Poor Miranda.

"Your mother would be ashamed of you, having a child out of wedlock..."

That gets my attention, even though I am 7 months pregnant and most of the time I waddle like a duck.

I won't sit back and allow my father try to guilt trip me by using my mother.

"Papa, please don't, am having a bad day and am not in the mood to. . . . ."

When he slaps me I don't feel it, I just feel the injustice of it all.

Here I am, crying inside, dying of heartbreak, wanting a little comfort from my father and this is what I get.

As I think about it, I start to get angry.

" Do not ever raise your hand at me again father, if you do not want me staying in your house you need only to say so and I would leave.

After all this is my country, I am pregnant, you have to deal if you want to be a part of my baby's life, I am not below disowning you, father dearest "

I say the last two part slowly so it would sink in.

I don't know why my father hates me, sometimes he acts like he cares and other times like he hates the very thought of me.

He just moves away and I know I have won this round.

Kismet 1 - Papa 0

I rub at my stomach when I feel my baby kick.

I smile, that feeling alone is worth what I have been through.

****

2 months later

"Mimi!"

"Calm down Kis, it will be over soon"

I breath in through my nose and out my mouth.

Oh sweet Christi it hurts.It hurts so much and I feel my chest clench like I have never felt before.

We've been at this for close to 12 hours now and I am so tired.

"The mother is going into shock"

I vaguely hear the nurse beside me say and I hear Mimi sob.

"Please Kismet, you have to try""Am so tired"I hear myself saying.

"Please Kiki, you have to try harder"She says, clutching my hand.

I shake my head slowly.I just want to sleep.

"She is bleeding, heart beat is faltering"

The nurse repeats and I hear the doctor say.

"Just one more push Kismet, just one more, help me bring your child into the world"

I nod.Just one, I can do that, just one.

I push with all my might and I hear the sweetest sound ever.The cry of my baby.

"And we have a little lady"

The doctor says and I give a little laugh even as I feel my strength waning.

"Can I hold her?"I say quietly.

"Please doctor, do something, my sister is dying"

I hear Mimi say but, I want to tell her am fine but I can't.

"Can I please hold my little Jasmin?"I ask again, I feel the nurses running around me but I concentrate all my attention on Jasmin.

"Is that her name kis? Jasmin? It's a beautiful name, you have to stay alive so we can take care of her together"

I hear Mimi say as if from a far place, I can hear the tears in her voice but I can't say anything.

I feel a tremor wrack through me and I cry out weakly.

I turn to Mimi even as I see the nurse take my daughter away to.

"You will take care of her won't you?"

I ask and she nods, crying.

Even as I drift away I think that this is the first time I have seen Miranda cry.

AN.Much love. Thanks for reading.

Chapter Eighteen

Ava MaxSweet but psycho

Same day as the birth of baby Jasmin.

Garrett.

"I don't understand what's going on boss, we searched everywhere, we have done everything possible but we still can't find the last member of the Osei's family"

Will says and I lift my head from dropping my boots.

"Where can a measly little girl hide?"

I ask Will and he takes a step back, he seems to get that I am beyond triggered.

I have succeeded in almost paying up my debts, I would have gotten on my mission of finding my girl if the idiots I worked with didn't do a sloppy job of reconnaissance .

How hard was it to find out how many members of a family there was.It's not as if you are the one doing the killing.

"Boss,am . . .""Just get out"

I say and he exits the room with all haste.I pick up my wallet and I get the picture of Kismet I have In it out.

In the picture she was smiling, it was the day she opened the flower shop,she was so happy that day.

My hand goes to my chest when I feel a ache there.Why does it hurt?

I go to stand up but I have suddenly lost all strength,I fall to the ground in the process upsetting everything on my desk.

It falls on the ground with a crash.I hear my door open and I hear Marcel's voice.

"Boss?""Get out"

"But. . .""Get the fuck out"

I say to him and he exits.If there is anyone I do not want seeing me weak it is Marcel.

That fucking backstabber.

I try to stand but I can't,I cry out when my chest gives a sudden ache.

I laugh humourlessly, is this how heartbreak feels?Is this how one dies of heart ache?

I roll on the ground and I curl up in a ball.How can I be so fucking weak.

I almost die when I feel tears slip down my eyes.

I think my eyes broke,my eyes are leaking.

I sob into my hand.God,I miss her so much,I miss her so damn much.

I sob harder and I pound on my chest.My chest is going to fall.

I think something is wrong, something is really wrong.

I think something is wrong with my Kismet..Nothing can happen to her, nothing.

I curl into a ball and I pray to any God that is listening.

Please,protect her, please protect my Kismet.At that moment I realized I would do anything for her.

Anything for my person.

I would give my life for her,she can have it.

I curl harder and I pray harder.

****At that moment, the man Garrett didn't realize the levity of what he did.He didn't realize the nature of sacrifice he made in keeping the girl Kismet alive.The greatest sacrifice of all.He gave up his life for his woman.

*****

Six years later.

Kismet.

I step out of the plane ,I take off my sunglasses, searching, looking around for that special person.

"Honey!"I lift my head at the voice and there she is.

"Mimi!"

I squeal before running down the ramp of the plane to her.She has balloons and everything with her and I jump into her arms,she commences to kiss my face.

I laugh as we twirl around like little girls.

When she stops she asks.

"Where's Jasmin?"I turn around and so does she,we watch as Jasmin walks to us ,he hands in Honey's.

"Oh my baby"Mimi squeals before kneeling down so that jasmin can run into her arms.My sweet girl doesn't hesitate because she does just that .

"Momma!!"

She squeals and I almost roll my eyes,my daughter has two mothers,I and my best friend.

"How's my baby girl doing?"She asks and Jasmin nods.

Mimi's eyes goes to were Honey is standing beside me.

"Who's this?"She asks, straight to the point.

"This is Honey"I say and she just lifts a brow, she is in protective mode.

"Who is Honey?"She asks in a prickly manner and I roll my eyes.

Ever since I died,yes died,she has been extra protective with a cherry on top.

Apparently after I gave birth to Jasmin I died for 2 mins 34 seconds.

Then I woke up,on my own,even after the doctor had announced the time of death.

The doctors called it a miracle,a spontaneous remission.

I think the sentence the nurse used was that it was as if my life was exchanged.

Like I had the angel of life there , breathing life into me.

I just believe that I wasn't meant to die then, I still have my life in front of me.

"Well, Honey is a friend I met in South Africa,she was coming to Nigeria and we decided to come together,we will be living together"

I say and Mimi gapes at me.

"Are you serious? How can you be so trusting?"She asks and I wince at her rudeness.

I open my mouth to speak but Jasmin beats me to it.

"I like her,she is nice and she gives me the best of chocolates"

Mimi fakes a smile before she speaks.

"Well, since my bunny can vouch for you I guess that makes it alright"

She says and I laugh.

"Let's go"She says and we turn to go but not before she throws me a look that says it wasn't over.

Sheesh.She still is as cold as ever.

AN.

You were scared right?Hehehe.

I know, I was scared too.Hope you have a great day today.Don't forget to comment.

Happy Halloween, enjoy!

Much love.

Chapter Nineteen

V incent The beauty inside

Kismet.

"It's totally fine Mimi, chill"

She looks appalled, she is still on my case with the Honey case.

"Don't tell me to chill, Kiki, just because you went on to SA to go on an energy cleansing trip in the mountains does not mean my energy is cleansed"

I roll my eyes as I push the tub of ice-cream towards her.

She woke me a while ago for this.

"You should get your energy cleansed"

I say to her.

"You did not just say that you"She says to me and I shrug.

"What's with you?, it's like you have no sense of self preservation, after all you went through, even the Garr..."

She stops herself when my eyes fly to hers, she winced, that's a forbidden name to mention in my presence and she knows it.

Not after everything I went through in the name of love.She clears her throat and opens her mouth to continue but I just cut her short.

"That's fine Mimi, what ever happens will be mistake to bear"

I say to her and she sighs."It hurts me when you make these mistakes and get hurt Kismet, don't be selfish, think about how I feel"

She says and it becomes weird for me, I don't know how to reply.Ever since the incident 6 years ago I find it hard to empathize with people.

It's like my feelings are bottled up or something, I even tried to talk to someone about it but it was useless.

Just made me hurt more and it was going no where.

I didn't have to bother though because her phone rings. I raise my brows, who calls a lady at…,i glance at the clock.

3 in the morning? Wow.

I take a bite of my ice-cream as I pretend not to listen to her conversation, although it's one-sided.

Mimi ;"What?" She asks the person on the other line, wow again, cold much?

Mimk; "It's 3 in the morning Jason, I told you my sister was coming to town didn't I?" Jason? Was that the….. Oh, naughty girl.

I smirk as I take another bite of my ice-cream.

Mimi; "I can't say that now Jason…" She listens some more before saying.

"Fine, I love you, goodnight or morning or night" I

choke on my spit and I cough so hard my eyes tear up.

She ends the call and looks at me unimpressed.

I get ahold of myself before saying. "I could have choked"

"You were fine, you wouldn't have choked" She says and am baffled.

"You were lovey lovey awhile ago, how can you be so cold to me? Your best friend and sister?"

"Just spit it out Kismet" She says in exasperation, massaging her temple.

"That was your boss right?" I ask.

"Give the woman a medal" She says sarcastically, I poke my tongue out at her.

"You are dating your boss? Good for you" I say and she finally cracks a smile.

"It's been 2 years now"

"What? You didn't tell me" "You didn't ask"

I shake my head, I know why she didn't tell me.

"I would have been happy for you Mimi, I am fine now"

I say and she nods, clearly not believing me.

"Really, I am fine, I am even dating now"

"You are?"

She asks surprised and I nod.

"I have a date in a week" "Are you serious? Are you going? With whom?"

I roll my eyes before replying.

"Yes, I am serious, yes I am going, why would you even ask that? And it's with the good doctor who saved my life"

"The good doctor is coming to Nigeria?" "it's not as if ghana is that far"

I say.

"No,No, I mean a guy is coming from another country to take you on a date, that's awesome, where would he stay?"

"Right here"

I say, trying to play it off, thinking she will be mad at me but she squeals.

I raise surprised eyes to her,Mimi never squeals.

"Why are you so happy?" "It's awesome to see you finally moving on"

I smile wanly at her and she squeals again.

I smile for real this time and we go back to our ice cream.

I don't bother telling her I haven't moved on at all, that sometimes when the pain is too much my chest hurts.

That most days I cry myself to sleep and that I take pills just to make me sleep.

That I have searched around for a replacement but it's as if nothing works.

She doesn't have to know that, she should believe that I have moved on.

My hand moves to my chest when I feel the familiar pain there.

I clench my other fist around my spoon as I swallow the pain.

This is nothing, most times I expect to see blood on my chest.

My eyes goes to Mimi and she smiles at me, unaware.

I smile back as I clench my fist tighter.

AN

Happy New month guys!! It's November, my birth month!!!

Are you surprised at how giddy I am? Don't be, am a cake freak and I don't always get to eat much of it.

But I promise to gorge on it on ya'lls behalf, hehe.

So it's on the 6th,my birthday that is, please wish me well, starting from today.

Kisses and hugs.

Muah!!!

Much love.

Chapter Twenty

C onor MaynardCrash

    Garrett.

My hand goes to my chest as I listen to will brief me on how the selling out of my business is going.

"Don't settle"I state and his head comes up startled.

"Boss?"

"I said don't settle, he can afford another few million dollars"

"But boss, this is a very good deal"He says and I raise a brow.

"You better not fucking settle, he's gonna accept the price we give, if you do, say good bye to both of your knees"

I say and he nods, bowing his head a little.

I wave him off and he exits the room, I make a mental note to keep my eye on the transactions, Will can be stupid at times.

I rest my head on my chair as I feel a migraine coming on.Shit.

I think back to the past few years, on how I have succeeded in cutting ties with the underworld.

I am now a honest to God clean business man.I have done everything in preparation for when I get my girl back.

Even after 6 years and 4 months her memory is still fresh in my head.I fist my chest when that darn pain starts again.

It won't be long now, I just have to find the last Osei's brat and I will be done with this life.

I will be free to get my girl.

I take a deep breath and I smell triumph I the air.

A knock sounds on the door.

"Enter"

My mom comes into view and I think.Oh fuck.

"You really are wicked Garrett Grayson"

"It's good to see you too maman""Phoo!"

She exclaims, I sigh, this will be long.

"You refuse to come see me, you are always too busy even for your mother"

"Maman...."

"I will kill myself if you don't agree to come see me soon"

"You won't Maman, you love yourself too much"

"You know me too well"

She says with a sigh.

"I miss you Gray, won't you do something for your Maman? Even Marc comes home every now and then"

The mention of his name sends my mood plunging and I sigh before nodding.

"You will come to dinner with me then? At the house?"

I nod again, when I cancel I will do it far away from the house.

"Promise me you won't cancel"

She says and I nod again.

"Good, see you later son, bye bye"

She says exiting in the same cloud of perfume as she came in.

I just roll my eyes.

Typical Maman, not once did she ask how I am doing.

-The god leza looked down at the male and sneered. Typical human, thinking he rules the world.

His fellow god watched him as he did so.

"Don't you think you are being too harsh? You know the Nigerian pantheon won't take it likely, they protect their own"

The god says and Leza sighs.

"It has to be done, it's the only way to atone my sins towards...."

"You think so? Don't you think you are actually confounding things by involving the Ghanaian and Nigerian pantheon?"

"Don't you think I have thought of that?"

He asks in anger and being the sky god the tress they stood on trembled against the sudden wind.

"Whatever you say Leza, just be careful, the Nigerian pantheon might eat you for breakfast"

..... Says before disappearing.

Leza turns, now alone with his thoughts his pain returns.

Why did he it have to hurt so much? After he fell in love with a human he couldn't protect, his chest had hurt after her death.

He beats on his chest as he vows to make this human who thought he was a god pay.

This human will be a scapegoat for the animal that killed his Sewa.

***

AN.

You don't understand? Please bear with me. Will explain in later episodes.

***Leza is the South African God of sky and creativity, (well according to Google)

I have added a link below of an article I think will be of help.

Apparently in the myth there was a woman who tried to climb to the heavens to ask Leza why she is going through so much sorrow as all her family members were killed.

She wasn't able to, she later fell to the earth and died of her sorrows.

I have romanticized it and made it in a way that the woman, Sewa was actually Leza's lover and he couldn't protect her and her family.

So his pantheon gods punished him to protect women forever.

I hope this was helpful. Please bear with me.

Muah..

http://www.mythencyclopedia.com/Le-Me/Leza.html

That is the link

Don't forget to tell me what you think. Like rate and comment.

Much love.

Pantheon:A temple dedicated to all the gods in a religion.

E. G

Olurun, orisha, sango, oya, etc. They are all gods of the Nigerian pantheon.

Chapter Twenty One

C loudRothy

Kismet.

"Am so nervous"

I roll my eyes."it's not as if you are the one going on a date, why are you nervous?"

"It's the first time you are going on a date in a while, I've got to be nervous"

"OK, keep on being nervous then"I lean closer to the mirror to make sure my mascara is not smeared.

"Did you make sure you didn't eat any garlic and onions?"

"Mimi, you literally made sure I ate nothing but cereal all day"

I smear some lip stain to my lips and I pucker them to tease her, she rolls her eyes.

"Did you wax?"

She asks and I roll my eyes for the thousandth time."No, I did not wax, I don't plan on sleeping with the guy on the first date"

"Why?"She asks, clearly appalled."it's, not as if you have anyone you are bumping uglies with"

She says and I nod my head slowly."You are right, I don't want to have sex with any one, well yet"

"Ohh, you naughty, naughty girl"She says and we laugh together.

"How do I look?"I ask, twirling around to make sure she gets the full effect of the gown.

I am wearing a gold dress with a plunging back, it makes me feel like a A-list actress.

"You look like a A-list actress""Ha!, my thoughts exactly"

I say and we laugh.Jasmin shows up at the bathroom door and I turn again to smile at her.

"Wow, mom, you look like an actress"See, great minds work together.

I bend to kiss her head and she giggles."Uncle Daniel is down stairs with Honey"

"He's here?, when did he arrive?""Just now, come"

She says, pulling me by my hand and I almost trip.My baby does not know it's a feat to run in 6 inches platform heels.

We get down stairs and there he is.I seriously don't know why I am going on a date with the guy any way.

It's not as if i like him, well I do like him, as I would like a brother but well....

"You look nice Kismet"

He says when I get to him and I nod, I can see Mimi watching us keenly and I make an effort to smile at him.

The girl can detect a fake date from a mile away, and seriously this is what this is, a big fake date.

She doesn't have to know that all we are going to talk about is how he will move onto one of lands my mom left me.

That he wants to move his practice to Nigeria and that I offered up my land for sale just as a gesture of gratitude.

She doesn't have to know.She should believe am moving on.

"Am going to wait up for you mom, with Honey"I nod at Jasmin.

"Have a good time Kismet"Honey says and I smile at her.

We begin to exit the room when Mimi speaks.

"Don't do what i wouldn't do".I throw her a look and she grins wickedly.

Daniel holds out a hand for me and I accept it, he open his car door and I get in.

Wow, spacious.

I think as I look around the interior of the vehicle.

"Is this a rental?"I ask him and he nods.

"It's nice"I comment.

"Thank you, I have a thing for cars"He says and I nod, we drive for a while so I ask a question just to break the silence.

"Where are we going now?" "I made reservations for us at an hotel, hope you will like it."

He says and I nod.

I can't help but think that doctor Daniel is a little bit boring.

We get to the hotel and we get valet parking.

He leads me to the entrance and immediately I pass the threshold I feel a cold draft around my body and I shiver.

My chest begins to ache and I come to a stand still. What's happening?

"Kismet? Are you coming?"

I see Daniel beckoning me from the hostess stand and I force a smile before gesturing for him to give me a minute.

I think...i think it's gonna be a long night.

****Garrett.

I throw Marcel a dark and if looks could kill he would be on the floor writhing, his innards boiling.

"Gray, darling, did you plan to stand me up?"

Maman asks as she peruses the hotel's wine list.

I left my house to this place to finalize a deal and after I get done my mother shows up just in time to stop from leaving. Shit.

"Never, Maman"

I say with my teeth clenched, I don't have time for this shit.

"Good, Marcel will be joining us for dinner" She says before signaling for a waiter.

I sigh as I massage my temple when I feel an headache coming on. Shit.

I look around as the waiter takes Maman's and Marcel's order.

I feel a cold grip me and immediately my heart starts to aches.

My hand creeps to it as I take a deep breath to settle, a flash of gold comes into view.

I don't know why it catches my eye but before I can concentrate the waiter blocks my view.

I let it go as I give him my order. Whisky, neat.

As the dinner progresses I find out what a disaster it was to think I could spend a whole hour with my mother and brother.

All she talks about is my step-dad and of course how she needs more money.

I don't respond, I just nod along and when she finishes her first course I stand, placing some bills on the table.

"Are you leaving Gray?" "Yes, maman, let's not do this ever again"

I say, throwing Marcel a look before walking away.

I didn't even get to drink my whisky, that's how much I hate my brother.

My hand goes to the necklace around my neck and I immediately feel better.

I go outside and wait for the valet to pull up my car. I feel a couple come to stand beside me and I pay them no attention.

"Are you sure you are okay? You look a little pale".

The man asks and I glance at my wrist watch. Where in hell Is the godforsaken valet?

"Am fine honey, it's just a little cold, nothing a warm cup of tea won't clear"

The female replies in a voice I know as I know mine and I freeze.

It can't be. It really can't.

I turn slowly but only catch a glimpse of her before she gets into the car a valet just pulled up in.

I immediately turn so she won't get a look at me and my brain begins to work.

Kismet, my Kismet is in Nigeria. She is only a breath away.

Her car pulls away and mine pulls in and that immediately sparks a thought in my mind.

Who is that she was with?

Chapter Twenty Two

T he Memory Of That Day

Kim Jong Wan

Garrett.

I follow them, (sorry Benedicta, your wish was not granted, hehe) I need closure.

My heart ached, longed for this woman for seven years and now she is right in front of me but with another man.

It can't be.

She promised to wait for me, she promised she will be mine for ever, she has to wait.

She has no other option.

I drive after them, I clench my fist around the steering wheel, my hand goes to the necklace on my chess t and I clench at it.

I follow them until they pull up into a Mcmasion in an estate, away from the rest of the world.

So this is where she thought she could hide from me? Can't say I am angry my mom conned me into staying for dinner with her.

I watch her get out of the car with the help of the man, my fist clench again.

If she is married, I don't know what I will do, I really don't know.My chest gives a pang and I acknowledge that for the first time I am in pain and I need my drug.

I need Kismet.

I begin to get out of my car but I freeze when I see Mimi and a little girl step out of the house.

The girl runs to Kismet who gives her a kiss on the head before lifting her hands up for the man who carried her in.

I take a broken step back when I feel pain like fire lance through my chest.

I cry out, and immediately I see Mimi turn around, I clasp my hand around my mouth as I stand still in the shadows.

My heart aches so much I feel my eyes water. I stand still and wait until Mimi enters the house.

I don't know how I drive back to my house, I don't know how I make it to the elevator or how I get into my room.

But I do know that I break down, I break down so hard that I feel a fever come up on my body.

I lie on my bed in pain in the darkness of my room and I close my eyes as the pain washes over me.

So.

The sun rises, it sets it rises again and I have no idea what the time is.

I shiver, I writh, I roll, turn, curl and finally I get up before padding to my bathroom to throw up.

I glance at my reflection on the mirror and I give a tired, slow smirk.

So this is what defeat tastes like? I go back to my bed and I lie still, taking a look at my life so far.

I don't regret what I have done so far, the only thing I regret is not meeting Kismet earlier in my life.

I lie for a while, I feel the fever wash over me and still I lie.

I have lost the will to live.

*****Kismet.

I groan and roll away form the cold towel.

"Don't do that" I say, swiping at Mimi's hand.

She sighs, exasperated.

"Just like you to return from a date with a fever"

"I was totally fine before.. It started as soon as I got to the hotel"

"Yeah, yeah, shut up and let me get a read on your temperature"

I quiet as she places the thermometer in my ear.

"Wow, this is pretty high"

She says as she removes it to look at Its reading.

After she makes me force down some pills and porridge I lie down.

The pills makes me groggy and I feel myself drifting.

"I don't even know why I am sick"

I say softly.

"Aww, my poor baby"

I hear Mimi say and I smile slowly.

"You know something Mimi?"

"Hmm mm, am sure you will tell me"

"I love you a lot"

"I love you too baby girl"

She says and I nod before continuing.

"I love Jasmin very much.... I also love papa, sometimes... I like Honey,.. She's a doll, a pretty lovely doll"

I say and I take a deep breath, she strokes my head and I close my eyes.

"You know who I love the most?..." I ask but I don't let her answer before i continue.

"I love Garrett, yeah, I really do, I know you never liked him,.... I know I was a naive little idiot...." I laugh humorlessly... "I really..really liked him.. I even slept with him after our second date.. That's how madly in love I was with him..."

I take a deep breath.

"I guess all I am trying to say is that.... I miss him, I really miss him Mimi, I miss his smell, his touch, his taste, every thing... I miss him Mimi"

I say and even though my eyes are closed I feel the tears seep out and I turn around, my back to her.

She doesn't say anything but I feel her get into bed with me, cuddling me, I still don't turn.

I don't cry, I feel so tired. I open my eyes to stare at the wall.

I feel defeated. So this is what defeat tastes like?I close my eyes as I try to find the will to live.

Chapter Twenty Three

S ay YesLoco

Kismet.

I shuffle down stairs in my jeans and off the shoulder sweater.

"Are you going out?"Honey asks me and I nod.

"Can you? Aren't you still sick?"

"Geez, thanks for the vote of confidence"

I say and she laughs, Mimi raises her head from some paper work.

"Where are you going to?" Mimi asks.

"The super market, we need groceries, since you decided to eat us out of the house, I have to restock"

She pokes her tongue out at me and I shake my head.

I turn to shout up the stairs at Jasmin.

"Baby girl, am about to leave, let's go"

"You are taking jazz?" Mimi ask and I nod.

Jasmin runs down the stair and I almost get an heart attack.

"Baby, never run down the stairs again ok?"

"Yes Maman, can we go now?" I roll my eyes, I don't know where she got that version of mother.

"See you later Mimi" Jasmin says and Mimi waves her on.

We walk outside and get In my convertible before driving to the local store.

"Moooom"Jasmin starts and I sigh before answering.

"You don't have to whine jazz, I can hear you just fine"

"You said we were gonna go to the big store"

"Well we are going to the local store, you know I am not too fine, I can't drive for long"

"Mommy.."

She starts and I know I have lost the game.

"Fine"

I say and I pull out of the local store's parking lot and we go on a drive.

"You are the best mom"

"I know, you should know that too" I say, flicking her nose and she giggles.

When we get there I pull into the last spot in the parking lot and we step out, I put on my sunglasses and Jasmin does so too.

I hold her hand as we walk towards the entrance of the mall. I try not to think of the last time I was here and how good the memories where.

I shake my head when they threaten to overwhelm me.

I grab a shopping cart and we begin to walk down the aisle. "Maman can i get some oreos?"

"Sure baby"I say as I peruse a brand of mints, it says on the label that it gives all day freshest goodness.

Am sure Mimi will appreciate the irony, I add it to the rapidly growing pile before I turn to Jasmin.

"Jazz baby, you can't have 9 packets of chocolates, put them back"

I say to her and she pouts but does as I say.

We go to the meat section and I get some beef, I am craving a little bit of suya, maybe I will barbecue some when I get home.

We get some ice cream and cheese before we go to check out.

Am standing behind a couple when Jasmin tugs on my sweater telling me that she just must have some s'mores, I nod and she runs away.

I keep my eyes on her and I see her grab a packet, my vision is blocked by a chest and I try to look past but stop when I feel that familiar ache in my chest region.

I dread lifting my eyes but I do and my world tilts on its angle.

So.

He is staring at me like he has seen a ghost, I can't help but try to take him all in at once.

He looks so good, a little pale but very good.

"Kis.." He starts in a broken whisper.

I turn when the checkout lady asks if I wanted to do a card or cash transaction. I hand her my card as I try to make my self forget what I just saw.

Jasmin comes to stand beside me and she hands me the smores, I take it and pass it to the checkout lady.

She swipes my card and bags my groceries, I take them and pull Jasmin with me.

"Careful Maman"

She says but I don't slow down, I don't even make it to the exit when his voice stops me.

It's official, I am a loser, a big fucking loser, and yes I just used a cuss word.

I can't believe even after all these years his voice still has the power to render me motionless.

"Maman? Why are we stopping?" Jazz asks and I pull her behind me as I turn, I see his eyes on jazz and I see pain lance through them and I immediately feel the urge to calm him.

Tell him everything was OK, I stop my self. It's no longer my right.

"Kismet.."

He starts and I open my mouth to speak but he falters before my eyes.

I frown, what's wrong? Is he sick?

"Baby, please let me.."

He starts again but stops and he staggers, I drop my groceries on the floor and I run to him when he almost drops to his knees.

The moment I make skin contact I feel at home, the pain in my chest goes away.

I lift my head when he tugs on my braid, I look into his eyes and he smiles a slow sad smile.

"Heaven baby, you touching me, it's heaven"

He says before passing out, I can't hold him up and we go down together. I begin to panic when I see the paper bag of drugs slip from his grip.

Is he sick? Is it serious? I hope.. I can't bear..

Not once did I think that he might be married and that I had no right to worry over him.

I try to get his phone from his pocket but there's none inside.

By now we've been surrounded by store goers.

"Please, somebody, call an ambulance!"

"I already did Maman, with your phone"

Jasmin says and I nod, I turn to Garrett on the ground and I stroke his hair off his face.

Before whispering.

"Please stay with me babe"

I say as I hear the sirens from the distance.

Chapter Twenty Four

S mile For MeSimi

Garrett.

I feel soft hands in my hair, it's soothing so I continue to close my eyes as I savor this moment of silence.

I try to remember what happened but I can't, I just remember that I was close to her.

To my Kismet.

My eyes flies open and I groan silently at the harsh light, I am In my room. Wait? My room?

I turn slowly and my eyes blur at the pounding headache in my head. It's Kismet, she's the one stroking my head.

I watch her as she unconsciously does it, I don't want to make a noise, I don't want to loose this moment.

She hums a tune, it's a familiar tune, I close my eyes to savor it.

"Maman, I think the man is awake" I freeze and so does the hand in my hair.

So it's true, my Kismet actually got married and had a child.

I sit up slowly and she watches me the way a sheep would watch a lion. With a lot of fear and a mix of fire.

I groan when I feel my head bang and she reaches out to touch me but I pull away.

Hurt flashes through her eyes and it kills me but I can't let her, she is someone else's.

My fist clench around the sheets and venomous thoughts pass through my head.

If it was another time I would have killed off the man and make her love me again.

"You don't have to look like you've seen a ghost Garrett" Her voice immediately soothes the beast in me burn her words gets me riled again.

"What are you doing here?" I ask her, albeit a little harshly.

"So you didn't switch apartments? You still live here?, thank God, it came in handy when I decided not to call your brothers, I knew you would hate that"

She says ignoring my question so ask my question again.

"What are you doing here?"

"I know you don't want to see me but you don't have to be so rude"

I raise a brow and although it costs me a little bit of my strength I don't let it show.

"What's that supposed to mean?"

She rolls her eyes and I stiffen, immediately going into gage mode.

"Did you just roll your eyes at me?"

She freezes, she knows how much I hate it. "I don't know, did I?" She responds and I vaguely see her child looking from me to her almost comically.

"Kismet, behave" That seems to get into her brain because she drops her sassy behavior and immediately adopts her ice cold persona.

I don't like that very much.

"How have you been Garrett?"

"What do you think?"

"You look good, you look more than ok"

"Well that makes one of us" I say leaning to extend my hand to the little girl, Kismet holds her back when she steps forward.

"What's that supposed to mean?" She asked, clearly in a tizz.

"Do you really want to do this?"

"I don't care if you are sick, I want you to explain what you meant by that"

"I am not sick" I deny, with conviction.

"Yes you are, the doctor said you had an high fever, Maman had an high fever too recently"

The kid says and my eyes goes to hers, it's as green as her mother's.

"The ambulance gave you an emergency procedure and brought you home, they say you should be better in a while"

She continues and I reply.

"If you say so then baby cheeks" I see Kismet look between us before turning to me.

"Explain Garrett" "Don't you think you we should say this without your child present?"

"Jazz, go to the sitting room and wait for me, don't touch anything"

"Maman?"

"Now, jasmine"

"Don't talk to her like that"

I state, she was being too harsh on the little kid, wait.

When did I loose my man card and started caring about kids?

Kismet doesn't say anything just throw the kid a look who exits the room quite quickly if you ask me.

"Are you a cruel mom? Does your husband know?"

I ask and she stiffens.

"I don't think you have the right to ask that Garrett, considering you didn't care seven years ago, I see no reason why you should be now"

"What do you mean?"

"I don't care to repeat my self"

"I didn't peg you for a flake hazel eyes"

"Don't call me that" "Why? Do you miss it?"

She tenses and take a deep breath.

"I absolutely despise you" She says and my hand goes to my chest where a pain suddenly develops, her eyes follow the gesture and I make an effort to drop my hand.

"Thanks for bringing me home Kismet, thank you for being here and not calling my brothers, I hope we don't meet like this again"

I say and she tenses.

"Are you asking me to leave your house?"

I don't reply, just concentrate on trying to stand.

She stands and picks up her bag from the floor.

The farther she gets away the harder it is to breath, I didn't think she would call my bluff.

But she is someone else's, I should let her go.

I walk behind her until she gets to the door of my bedroom where she stops.

"Asshole"

What?

"What?"

I ask.

"You are an asshole"

She says and I can hear the tears in her voice.

"Hazel eyes...."

Her tears totally kills me.

"I waited for you, you promised me you would always come back, I waited, I even tried to make it easier on you so I tried to find you and still you didn't want me"

"What are you talking about Kismet.."She turns and I can see the rage in her eyes.

"You didn't want me, you threw me away, I needed you but I couldn't have you, you didn't let me have you

You were mine Garrett! Mine!"

"I was all yours Kismet, but when I really needed you to trust me you threw me away first, I really need you Kis, I needed you like I needed my next breath"

"I was young, I was being threatened!"

"What?" I ask? Calming down even as the headache in my head fights to take me down.

"It's all in the past now"

She says, cleaning her face, drying her tears.

"Kismet..."

"Good bye Garrett, let's never meet again"

She says, her hand going to the door knob.

"Hazel eyes, won't you stay?"

I ask, using the line from her favorite telenovela.

"You don't get to use that line Garrett, I miss you and I still love you but you don't get to use that line".

"You miss me? You love me?" Finally the ache in my head recedes.

"Good..."

"I missed you too, I missed you very much, so much that my heart ached when I was away from you"

"Mine too"

She admits, finally turning fully to take a step towards me.

I close the distance.

"Please Kismet, for the sake of my sanity, please tell me I made a mistake the other night and you are not actually married"

"Other night?"

She asks in confusion.

"Kismet.."

"What ever gave you the thought that I was ma...."

I didn't let her finish before I bend down to kiss her. For the first time in 7 years I feel at peace.

Fuck. This woman is my home.

I break the kiss, resting my head on hers.

"I missed you, I fucking missed you so much baby girl"

"I missed you too big guy"

I kiss her head, placing it on my chest and she wraps her hand around me. We stay like that for a while before I ask.

"Who is Jasmin?".

She tenses and I think that I won't like her answer.

AN.

Consider giving this chapter a vote.

And thank you!

Chapter Twenty Five

Goodbye Wendy

Kismet.

I knew it was only a matter of time before the truth of Jasmin's father came out.

I always thought that it would be Jasmin asking the question not Garrett.

Freaking Garret.

He watches me now wearily as if bracing his self for a heart wrenching news.

And heart wrenching it would be.

"Kismet?" "Garr...."

I start and he interrupts me.

"Were you married? Did you have a child? You can tell me baby"

He says and I blink the sudden rush of tears away.

In hindsight I could see I was selfish, keeping the truth of my pregnancy away from him but I was young and naive.

I was scared, I had no one, and the thrill of having a first boyfriend and then finding out he might be a potential armed robber was just too much.

I shake my head no to his earlier question before I speak.

"Garret, you have to understand that I was scared, I had no one, I had thought that you had left me"

"What are you talking about Kis?"

"Garrett....."

He looks closely at me, waiting for me to say something but am scared, he seems to come to a realization.

"Is... Is Jasmin mine?"

He asks in a broken whisper and I sob a little before nodding. He takes a step away from me and I rock a little at the sudden pain in my chest, he stops.

"I had... No.. I have a child?"

He asks and I nod. He doesn't reply, just opens the door and walks to the sitting room.

This few moments of me waiting for his reaction is killing me. Am dying a slow death.

Jasmin looks up from the couch where she has found a Rubik's cube to keep her company.

"Are we going home now Maman? Am hungry, there was nothing in his fridge"

She says, throwing an accusing look at Garrett.

Garrett chuckles brokenly as If in awe and I think how great a mistake it would have been if this day didn't happen.

"Can we go now?" Jazz asks and I shake my head.

"I have something to tell you jazz girl"

I begin, preparing my self to shatter my daughter's world.

"No, it's fine, she doesn't have to know yet"

Garrett says, interrupting me.

"We can prepare lunch for you jazz, can I call you Jazz?"

Garrett asks and my daughter.. No...our daughter and she nods.

"Wait... Since am a guest can we order pizza?"

She asks Garrett with a mischievous smile and he smiles.

"You are a cheeky one aren't you?... Sure, let's order pizza and cola, sounds great?"

Jazz nods and I beam, I send Garrett a concerned look when he wavers.

His whole demeanor made me forget that he was actually sick.

"Are you ok?" I whisper to him

"We can go home and come back tomorrow"

He shakes his head.

"I missed seven years of you and my child, I don't want to miss a second more, I will be fine"

He says and I nod.

He bends to kiss my lips when jazz turns away and I am content.

*****

Garrett.

The look on Mimi's face was beyond comical, I know she thought she had seen the last of me but think again.

"What are you doing here?" She immediately asks as I help Kismet bring in her groceries the next morning.

Kismet had called her the previous night telling her not to worry, that she was OK.

Am sure she never thought that Kismet would be with me not to talk of show up with me today.

"Mimi, you know my new friend?" Jazz asks and its looks a feat to see her struggle to fake a smile.

"Yes baby, why don't you go upstairs to honey so that the both of you can get you ready for piano lessons? Uh?"

I don't take my eyes off her and Kismet begins to look between us.

"You guys please, don't start this nonsense again guys, am too happy for you both to ruin it"

Kismet says and Mimi pulls up her fake smile, Kismet nods before taking some groceries to put away.

"Now tell me what the hell you are doing here?"

"What? You didn't miss me?"

"You broke my friend's heart you fucktard"

I smirk.

"Is that why you lied to her about contacting me?"

"That's besides the point,.. She was heartbroken, she was going to move on... You couldn't come back and ruin it"

I feel rage settle on my skin like ice.

"Ruin it?" I ask and she instinctively takes a step back, good, am in a mood to break her fucking neck.

"I would have been here to take care of my woman if you didn't fucking lie to her, I would have been with her through the many morning sicknesses, through the labor, through the baby shower and every other fucking thing.

I missed my child's birth, I missed her taking her first step, I missed her saying her first words, I missed her going to school for the first time, she must have been bloody scared, I missed her taking swim lessons, I missed her taking piano lessons, I missed her first recital, I missed her first laugh, her first smile, her first tooth, I fucking missed every thing so don't you stand there all high and mighty with your judgemental bullshit and tell me how I ruined a life, you Miranda, you ruined a life, you are the most fucking selfish bitch I have bloody met, I only leave you alive because my woman loves you, don't try to pull one over me again because trust me I would kill you, I promise you I will"

I say with all my pent up anger, it's a miracle that I am still speaking calmly.

"Don't you fucking try to tell me off Garrett Gage Grayson, who do you think you effing are? Are you mad? Do you think I know nothing about your little spree in south Africa? How bloody hypocritical can you be? You don't get to come here and act like you are dad of the year, you are a killer

Garrett, a fucking mercenary, you don't deserve any of them, you deserve to die alone "

She says and I begin to understand how true her words her.

I don't deserve Kismet, but I will be damned if I walk away from her again.

She has accepted me without even caring about my secret and my flaws , I will be with her if it's the last thing I do.

"Get out"

I whip my head towards the kitchen and I see kismet standing there.

Oh shit, how much of our conversation did she here.

I begin to take a step towards the exit when she speaks.

"Not you Garr, Miranda, get the hell out"

"Kiki..."

"He deserves us, and he doesn't deserve to die alone so get out, am too angry to see you right now"

She says before turning to walk back to the kitchen. I stand still. But I can't help being smug.

Garrett : 1 - Miranda ; 0

Ha.

AN.

Don't forget to vote and comment.

Chapter Twenty Six

Suran   Wine.

Kismet.

I feel him rather than see him enter the kitchen with me and I try to make my self look busy as can be.

Am so angry right now that I could kill... No wait.. Hurt.. On second thought, never mind.

I turn to Garrett before lightning into him. Am as angry at him as I am at Mimi.

"Do you let her talk to you like that?" "Baby..."

"Ha... I am so speechless right now, I mean, I know she is my sister and all but you don't let her walk all over you, no one gets to walk all over you Garrett"

"Am guessing you only entered for the last part of her speech, trust me baby girl, no one can walk over me, even your sister.

I and her might have our misunderstandings but it's between us, it doesn't have anything to do with you.

You have to go talk to her "

" No am not going to, you don't have to be kind or anything "

"Trust me darling, am not being kind, am just looking out for you, I know you, I know you would regret your rash decision in approximately 3 minutes"

"I won't regret it, I won't feel bad" I say but I know it's a lie, I am already feeling bad.

He just raises a brow and looks at me intently.

"OK, fine, I will apologize but not yet, I want her to suffer a bit"

"Ha, good, my baby has a bad side to her now"

"Your baby is Badass now" I say with a cheeky smile.

He strokes my hair as he comments. "My baby has a potty mouth too, she now uses cuss words"

"I picked up a thing or two over the last few years"

"Can't wait to discover them" He says and I rest my head on his chest and we stay like that for a while.

"Garrett?"

"Hmm?"

"You can't bring your brother and your friend close to my family again"

He tenses and I wait for him to ask for and explanation but he just acquiesce.

"OK baby"

He says and I want to ask why he doesn't ask bug I don't, I guess maybe he has his own suspicions too.

"Garrett?"

"Hmm?"

"Am so glad to have you back"

"Yeah baby"

We stay like that for a while and he strokes my hair for a while too.

*****

Garrett.

"You can't open your eyes, okay?"

She nods with a disgruntled look on her face.

Kismet giggkrs beside me before commenting.

"Jazz hates surprises" "She will love this one"

"Really Garrett?"

"Yes baby girl"

"Can I see it now?"

"No darling, follow me"

I say as I lead her towards the house.

We've thought about this at length, getting a house for the two of us and finally we settled on the beach house.

It's every thing Kismet wants and Jasmin too.

We want to start as a family, far away from my family and everything.

I would be the one facing the unholy side of things, I don't want my family leaving me again.

We are going to be together, forever. Trust me. I can make that happen.

I remove the blind fold from jazz's and she blinks.

"What are we doing here?"

"It's our house" I say to her.

"Really? She asks with all the excitement in the world"

"Yes darling"

"Wow"

She squeals before running inside and we laugh and follow.

"No running jazz"

Kismet says and I shake my head at her.

"Let her be, it's childproofed" She turns to me and smiles.

"You thought of everything didn't you?"

"Yes baby, everything for you and jazz"

"I'm gonna tell her today" "You sure?"

I ask, am totally fine with jazz thinking I am her mom's new boyfriend, no need to tip her life on a balance.

"It's fine, we gave birth to a strong girl"

She says before standing on her tippy toes to kiss me.

I kiss her back and things get hot pretty fast.

I break the kiss before speaking in her ear.

"We should probably find her and show her the music room"

I say and we hear a squeal.

"Uh? Seems she found it already"

A flying body runs down the stairs and I catch it as it flies at me.

"You are the best ever Garrett!!!"

"Can I get a kiss for being the best?"

She kisses me smack on the lips and I laugh at Kismet wide eyes.

"You are the best Garrett".

She repeats and I kiss her hair,i reach a hand out for Kismet and she comes, we stand in front of the bay windows and look out at the sea.

Am content.

AN.

Am sorry, am really sorry.

I had things to do and that's why I slacked a little.

Enjoy this for the afternoon, will get back to you in the evening.

Much love.

Chapter Twenty Seven

S ean PaulGlue

Kismet.

I wakeup to kisses trailing down my back, I sigh and turn over.

"Good morning"

I sigh again into his mouth when he brings his lips to mine.

We share a kiss and he nuzzles my neck, I giggle.

"Some one seems happy"

I say to him and he nods, pulling my front to his.

"Am very happy, I'm ecstatic, I have you, I have our child, am more than happy"

When he says things like this, it makes me fall deeper in love with me.

"You are a sweet talker you knlw that?" "Only for you hazel eyes"

He says before kissing my shoulder then he gets serious.

"How do you think she is handling it?" "Handling what?" I ask jokingly and he bites my shoulder and I squeal.

I settle back on his chest before getting serious.

"I think she is perfectly okay with it, she loves you, she loves me, she wants to make us happy, so she is happy"

"Yeah?"

He asks, rubbing his stubble on my face and I close my eyes before nodding.

We are quiet for a while before I say.

"You should really shave, you are giving me beard burns"

"Yeah?"

"Uh uh, you want me to do it for you?"

"Can you?"

I turn to him.

"I can try"

He smiles and lifts me up, bedsheets and all to the bathroom and I squeal.

"Garret!!!"

"Hush" He says before setting me on my feet and then preparing the necessary things to shave.

He seats onto the jacuzzi and I stand between his legs.

"My face is all yours"

He says and I poke my tongue at him.

I smear shaving cream on his face and I begin to shave in the direction of his growing hair.

When am done I wipe his face with a warm towel and he turns his face to look at the mirror.

"Wow, my baby got skills"

"I used by to watch papa shave every morning when mom was still alive."

I say and he tugs on my hair, bringing my lips to his.

I kiss him hard before straddling him. He lifts his head to bite my cheek and I close my eyes.

"I love you" He whispers in my ear and I smile.

"I know"

"Do you want to explore the new bed?"

He asks with a cheeky smile and I laugh.

"I thought you would never ask"

I say and he carries me back to the bed and soon enough we begin our exploration.

*****

Garrett.

"Where are you Garrett?"

"Is there a reason you are speaking to me informally?"

I ask the receiver on the other line and I hear him take a deep breath.

"Gage you don't understand, you are not done with your job, how can you go incognito? The Osei's family will eat you alive"

"How is that your business Marcel?"

"You don't get to do this Gage"

"You don't get to tell me what to do and not to do Marcellus"

"Gage!!"

He growls and I growl right back.

"Marcellus Grayson, so help me God if you do not defer to me right now I will have your head!"

He is silent for a while and a noise brings my head up, Kismet is dancing with Jasmin by the ocean.

I lie back on the beach towel. I feel peace run through me and I settle.

Marcel speaks again.

" You are with her aren't you? "

" Marcel... "

" Gage, you fool, don't do this"

I frown.

"Marcel...."

"Gage, let her go, her and her child, let them go.. If you really want to protect them you have to let them go"

I feel black come into my vision. I feel rage course through me and I clench my fists.

"Marcel, you do not talk about child or my woman, the next time you do, I will have your head"

I say to him before disconnecting.

I clench my fist more and I get the urge to hit something but I lift my head and I see Kismet waving and smiling at me.

I immediately fall back down.

I'm fine, I have my family, I am fine.

I say this to myself for a while and still I can't settle,

I know what I have to do, i know but I still deny it.

Kismet is walking towards me and she looks marvelous in her sarong and bikini.

She is smiling when she sits between my legs and kisses my chest.

"Hey babe"

She says and I kiss her temple and she settles into my arm and we watch Jasmin build a sandcastle.

I Finally admit to my self that I know what I have to do.

I have to complete my mission and then cut my self off from that part of my life.

I have to do that to protect my family.

I have to be a monster again.

AN.

Hey hey hey.

Good morning, how ya'll.

Thanks for reading and please remember to vote and comment.

Much love.

Chapter Twenty Eight

I Won't StopChris Brown

Garrett.

"Faster daddy, faster!"Jasmin squeals at me as I run after Kismet.

"She's going to get away!"Jasmin laments.

"Ha, you can't catch me!"Kismet shouts at me and for the millionth time I wonder what brought me into this game of theirs.

I throw more pillows at her and Kismet dodges every one of them.

Tell me again please, which one of us is an assassin and is well versed in MMA?

" Slow pokes, am gonna get upstairs and steal all the gems, muah ha ha ha"

OK, she has the evil laugh down pat..Apparently my daughter is rapunzel and Kismet is the evil witch, am trying to stop the witch from getting the gems that will free rapunzel from the tower.

What am I supposed to be?Prince charming?

"Kismet, hold on, just let me catch you"

"It doesn't work like that daddy, you have to catch her and slay her with your big shiny sword!"

I have a big shiny sword?

"Hahaha, you can never catch me.!"Kismet laughs evilly.

I roll my eyes, fascinated albeit a little tired of this game.

"Kismet baby...""Who is this Kismet you are talking about?"

Kismet asks me and I sigh, she continues.

"Show her to me so I can steal her beauty too, I'm the evil witch.. Haha haha"

OK, that didn't work.

"Evil witch baby, come closer let the dashing prince give you a big shiny kiss"

She falters and I know I have caught her.

"Come on, you know you want it, come on"

She takes a step close and I close the distance, kissing her deeply.

"Eww, that's gross, and secondly, Maman, you are a flake, and daddy! Am supposed to get the kiss!"

"You want a kiss baby girl?"

"Uh huh"

She says nodding and I smile, letting go of Kismet to pick her up.

I kiss her eyebrows first and then kiss her cheek and then her head before lastly pecking her lips.

"Happy?"

"I'm hungry"

She says and I laugh.

"Okay, come on, let's have lunch, uh?"I ask and she nods again.

I lead her and Kismet to the dinning where she already prepared lunch.

"What's for lunch?"

It's obvious that it's beef stew and potatoes but my baby likes asking that?

Apparently she watched a movie were the cat always asked, what's for lunch?

"It's beef stew and potatoes baby, your favorite"

"But I wanted noodles"Jasmin whines.

"You can't have noodles young lady, you had that this morning"

Kismet responds.

"But..."

"That's enough Jazz." Kismet says again

"Daddy!"

"Eat your potatoes baby girl, we will have pizza for dinner okay?"

"Really daddy?"

"Yes baby" She stands up to kiss my cheek before whispering into my ear.

"I love you more than mommy,"

"I love you too" I whisper back and Kismet rolls her eyes.

She heard.

It's something they do when they are angry at each other, they automatically stop loving each other more.

We begin to eat and I slip forkfulls of beef into Jasmin's mouth.

When we are done Kismet produces ice-cream cakes and Jasmin squeals.

"I love you mommy!"

"I love you too baby girl" Kismet responds and jazz smiles, teeth stained with icing

The door bell rings and I get up to get the door.

"It's alright, I will" Jasmin says before zooming away.

I settle back into my chair and wait.

She doesn't show up for a while and I get a bad feeling.

"Jazz dear, who is at the door?"

Kismet shouts and no response comes, I feel dread run through me and I go to stand up.

"It's was just a man, he brought this"

She says stepping into the dining, raising a package and I feel relief course through me.

"It's addressed to you daddy".

She says, climbing onto her chair before passing the envelope to me.

I accept before turning to her.

"On no account baby girl should you answer the door or open it to any stranger okay?"

"Yes daddy"

She says swinging her legs, licking her fork and I don't think she gets it.

"Do you understand me Jasmin?"

"I understand you daddy"

"Good" . I lift my head to see Kismet watching me.

"Who is the package from?"..

She asks and I just smile.

"I'm sure it's something from work, don't bother your self"

"You sure?" She asks and I nod.

"OK baby"

She says before dipping her fork into her cake and taking a bite.

My eyes go to the package and I know, I just know it's something bad.

AN

Heya, this one is for my one day hiatus.

Am sorry, I was having writer's block.

Please don't forget to like rate and comment.

Much love.

And also, there's a new episode on wattpad on howl.

Remember to read it, my user ID is Bebe_Ernest.

Please give me a follow if you are on wattpad. Xoxo.

Chapter Twenty Nine

A m I Wrong Nico & Vinz

Garrett.

I put her to bed and I lean to kiss her head distractedly, she frowns at me before snuggling deeper into the pillow.

"Aren't you coming to bed yet?"Kismet asks and it brings me back to the present.My thoughts have been plagued by what might be in the package delivered.

I shake my head at her earlier question and she let's me go.I turn around to leave but her voice stops me.

" You will tell me if something is wrong, right Garrett?"

"Yes baby"I say, the lie smoothly rolling off my tongue.She nods and then closes her eyes before sleeping.

I wait until I am sure she is deep in sleep before slipping out of the room.

I walk to the dining and sit on one of the chairs, I rip open the envelope with a letter opener.

Inside are photos of Kismet and Jasmin, many different photos.

I go through all of them as I feel fear course through me, the photos are so clear that it is obvious the person who took them was in a close distance to them.

I clench my fist.Something more could have happened, he could have done something more.

For the thousandth time I feel hate at Marcel course through me.

Inside the envelope there is a note.

If you want to keep your family picture perfect, finish your job.

There is no signature, no other mark and I realize.

We might not be as safe as I thought, I clench my fist.

Where is that Osei brat hiding?

******

Garrett.

"I have no idea why you wanted us to end our vacation early"

Kismet says as she buckles Jasmin in.

"I'm sorry baby, duty calls, promise to make it up to you"

"Oh? Really?"

"Yeah, really"

I say and she goes on her toes to kiss me.

I return the kiss back, I just have this nasty feeling in my stomach.

"Get in the car baby girl"

I say to her and she does so, I throw Jasmin a wink and throws me a disgusted look.

She hates any form of PDA.

I get in the car and back out of the beach house, we are on our way to the house Kismet owns.

I need help in protecting them and I plan on asking Mimi for said help.Ha, how the mighty has fallen.

I have to know they are protected before I can leave on finding the Osei vermin.

"When are we going to go back to the beach house daddy?"

Jasmin asks from the back seat and I meet her eyes in the rear view mirro r."Very soon baby girl"I respond.

"And we are going to go together? You, mommy and I?"

"Yes baby"

"You promise?"

"With my heart soul and body"

"You are the best in the world daddy!"

"Don't you forget that"

I look at Kismet and I see her smiling at us.

I clench my fist around the steering wheel, I can't get over how beautiful she looks.

She places her hand on my thigh and I rest my hand on hers.

"I love you Garrett"

"I love you Kismet"She smiles before looking out the window.

*****Garrett

"So let me get this straight.., you are asking me for my help?"

"Yes" I answer plainly, it's taking a lot of my restraint to stand here and ask Miranda for help.

I will do anything for Kismet and my child, loosing my pride is one of them.

"You want me to protect Kis and Jazz?"

"Yes again"

"Why?"

She asks dubiously.

"Please, just trust me? Yeah?"

"That's a big request coming from you Garrett"

"Miranda, let's set aside our differences and ally now, we both want Kismet to be safe, let's do that,deal?"

She eyes me for a while before taking the hand I have outstretched.

Footfalls on the stairs bring my head up and I see a girl standing there with a mug.

She looks startled to see us there.

" I'm sorry, I didn't know any body was awake, I just want some juice"

Mimi turns to her and asks.

"Can't sleep Honey?"

"Yeah, insomnia is a vile thing"

She says, her eyes coming to me.

I watch her as she pours some juice and I try to understand what about her looks so familiar.

"Well goodnight". She says, leaving Mimi and I standing there.

"What's that look?"

Mimi asks and I shake my head.

"Where do you say the girl.. Honey is from again?"

"Why? Why do you want to know?"

"She looks very familiar, s'all"

"Well am sure it's because you've seen her around the house, she is Kismet's friend, a very cool chick"

I nod my understanding and she rolls her eyes.

"Well goodnight"

She says, leaving me standing there.

I frown, trying to remember, I'm sure I have never seen her before today.

And the look she gave me, what was that about?

I juggle my memory but nothing comes, I try to forget by thinking about the Osei brat and finally, finally I get it.

Oh shit.

I storm upstairs to her room.

I fling the door open and there she is, trying to jump out the window.

I pull her back, staring into her eyes, the same eyes I have seen in countless of different men and women as they loose the life in them.

"Why are you here?"

*****AN.

Heya, good afternoon.

How are you?

So, enjoy this for the afternoon, will be back in the evening. Don't forget to like, rate and comment.

Muah, kisses!!

Chapter Thirty

No song Today.

Garrett.

"Let me go you asshole!"

She whisper yells at me and I can't help but be amazed.

She was right in front of me all this while, here I was searching for a girl that might as well mean my salvation and she was here, bunking with my wife.

"I won't ask again, why are you here?"

"What do you think you buffoon? Yo killed my family, don't you think it's right that I kill yours?"

I growl as my hand goes to her neck.

"It seems you didn't get the memo, you girl are going to die, sooner or later"

"Oh really? Do you think your darling naive Kismet will be able to accept that the father of her child is a murderer? An assassin? A mercenary?""You talk too much for a roadkill, girl"

"My name is not girl, my name is Stephanie"

"I don't care, you are leaving this house here and now"

"Trust me, you won't want that" She says with so much conviction that I frown.

"What's that supposed to mean"

"A life for a life Grayson, a life for a life"

"You are mad" I say as she spouts rubbish from her mouth.

"Am I? Am I really?"

"What's that supposed to mean?" I ask, the fear in my belly spreading.

I look into her eyes and I see nothing, no emotion, no fear, no sadness, no remorse, nothing.

Normally when my victims find out who I am they get scared, this... This girl is showing no emotion, it's.. its different.

"As much as I love your wife and her child, I love my life just as much, I don't want to die, you are blind of you don't see what is right I front of you"

"What?"

"You priceless fool.. You think you know it all, you think you have everything in control but you don't, there are powers greater than you"

I'm tired of this rubbish, I don't want to hear more.

I pull her hand to get her to move and finally I see the panic in her eyes. "Don't you want to know?"

"Know what?"

"Know how you or Kismet is going to die"

I squeeze her hand and she cries out. "Kismet has my protection, nothing is going to happen to her"

"Then will nothing happen to you?" "What are you on about, speak plainly"

"First of all, you have to find out the traitor in your camp"

"What do you know about that?" I don't know why I am asking her so many questions but....

"It's a smoke and mirror's life you are living, taking a risk, living on a dare, what seems right is not how it is ad what seems wrong might very well be a treasure to you"

I am getting tired of this. "Girl,!..."

"Just find out Garrett, I won't be living, I will be here, smiling into your face when it comes crashing down"

I watch the malice in her face and I take a step back.

"Tell me what you have done"

"Oh, it isn't me, it's my guardians, they are watching over me"

I shake my head whamen I feel a fog cover my vision.

I feel my chest clench in that painful way and I groan.

"It's starting"

"What's starting??? Tell me you...."

I cry out again.

"What you wished for the most, it's starting..."

I look into her eyes and I see sympathy there and I feel cold, so cold.

I stumble out of her room into the hall way and I make my way to Kismet's room.

I see her curled on the bed, sleeping, I nearly breath a sigh of relief but stop.

She is whimpering, curling into herself, curling into a ball.

"Kis??"

"It hurts Garrett"

She says, still not opening her eyes. I climb into bed with her and I feel the pain lessen.

She immediately breaths a sigh of relief before curling into me.

"Better baby?" "Hmm hm" She mumbles and I kiss her head.

She drifts off and I don't, I stay up thinking how what I am thinking is impossible.

How I am going to have to kill one of Kismet's friends.

I sigh as I curl into her after a while.

It's a hard life I'm living.

AN. I know, I know you are probably angry at me and am sorry.

I'm really sorry, infact I'm crying.

I promise to update another chapter this afternoon, already working on it.

Beautiful Mess is coming to an end. I know, it's painful.

Thanks for reading, please don't forget to like rate and comment.

Thanks sweetness.

Chapter Thirty One

G arrett.

I watch her as she makes breakfast, she wipes a hand over her brows and for the fifth time this morning I catch a wince

"Are you okay mom?"Jasmin asks and that gets everyone at the breakfast table's attention.

"Yes sweetheart, am.just feeling feverish, I will take a pill and feel better"

Jasmin nods before turning to me."Are you going to be around when I get back today daddy?"

"I don't think so baby, I have things to attend to, but I will be around for dinner"

"OK, get me Popsicles when you are coming"

"Sure thing baby girl"I smile at her before turning my attention to Kismet.I see her waver.

"Maybe you should seat down love? Yeah?"

"I don't know why am suddenly feeling like this, I was okay until last night"She says.

"Maybe it's something you ate"Mimi says and Kismet nods.

"Maybe, I'm gonna rest up for a bit"She says and I turn my attention to Honey to see her already looking at me.

I just know she knows what this is about.I pull Kismet to me and she comes willingly.

"Take care of yourself baby, will take care of you when I get back"

"Where are you going to?"

"Promise to tell you when I return"I say and she nods, I vaguely see Mimi's attention fly to me but I don't turn.

I kiss Kismet on the lips before bending to kiss jazz.

I exit the room but not before throwing a look at Honey.

She stars back in defiance and I feel my fist clench.

I will take care of her when I get back, first things first.

****I drive to my former base and I get out of my car, making sure to cross check the glock in my waist band and the pistol in my jacket.

I take a look around, trying to make sure that I am not caught unawares by any surprises.When I find none I make my way inside.

Marcel greets me.

"About damn time you showed up"He says by way of greeting and I punch him when he gets close enough.

"What the hell Gage?!! Shit man, that hurts!"

"I turned a blind eye to everything you were doing Marcel, I fucking let you off the hook every single time! Then you go on to threaten my family?"

"What are you talking about Garrett?"He says, cleaning the blood from his nose.

"You made Kismet leave me 7 years ago, you made me loose precious time with my child and still I let you off because of maman and you still go on to betray me?"

"Garrett...."

"You will regret everything Marcel, you have been disowned by me!"

"Garrett!.."He starts and I pull him by his collar to punch and he takes it.

I scoff.

"Weak, you are so fucking weak.."I say and still he doesn't say anything, I tire of this.

"Fight! Fight! Marcel, fight like a man!""I don't want to fight you Garrett"

"FUCKING DO IT!"

"SHUT UP!! SHUT UP GARRETT!! SHUT UP AND FUCKING LISTEN!"

He shouts and I still, Marcel has never sounded this venomous.

He begins to laugh, staggering back, laughing like a maniac.

"You fool, you priceless, useless fool!"He says and that's twice in one day, I tire of it.

"You think you know it all, you think you are so well protected, you think that and yet you don't see what's right in front of you, glaring at you!"

"Marcel...!!"

"Shut up and listen!!! Shut the bloody hell up!!"

He says before continuing."I am your brother, I would never betray you, I would never hurt you, I love you, I fucking love you with all my heart and I will remain loyal to you until I die but Garrett... Fucking see what is in front of you"

When he says this I feel a terrible feeling in my stomach, I feel cold.

"What do you mean Marc?"

"I protected you when you were injured in SA, I protected you when Will, bloody Will tried to see you to the Osei's, I tried to protect Kismet from him too, your child I found ou and scare her away.. It was to make sure you weren't hurt.

It was to make sure that you were OK... I tried to tell you countless times but he held my girl over me like a dark cloud.

Yes Garrett, I was in love too but gave it all up for you.Will is the traitor here, think about it.

He's jealous of you, think about it, how's he's always there when you don't even know you need him, how's he's always trying to piant me in a bad light.

fucking see the hand writing on the wall Garrett "

I take a step back as he hits me with this information.

" He made a deal with the shaw's, he was going to make you their killing machine all that he could take over your territory here in Nigeria.

Don't you see it?!!"

He asks again but I don't have time to acquiesce when a voice calls from my back..

"He's right Garrett.. And a good thing too, I am soo tired of sucking up to you"

He says in a playful maniacal voice and I feel a cold in my stomach.

How could I have been so stupid?

"Will..."

"So what will it be then? You first or your brother dearest?"He asks pointing his gun at me and I pull Marc behind me.

"Well Will, I pick none of those options"

Chapter Thirty Two

J ason Derulo   Trumpets

Kismet. "Are you sure you are okay?"Mimi asks and I nod.

I feel a massive headache and I massage my head, it's been long I felt this way, I remember feeling like this only when I was pregnant with Jasmin.

"I think I should lie down" I say to no one exactly.

"Yeah, I think maybe you should" Mimi says.

"No stay awake, you can't sleep off a migraine" Honey says and I nod, I rest my head on my hand.

"Let me tell you a South African folk tale" "How's that going to help?" Mimi asks shrewdly and I rest my hand on top of hers.

"It's fine Honey, I want to hear, please tell me, anything to take my mind off this headache"

She nods and she begins.

"Once there was a god called Leza, he was the god of creativity and air, he was a kind god albeit stand offish, he took care of his people and made perfect decisions and balance.

Everything was that way for a thousand years until he fell in love. You know how love can ruin perfect balances right?. That was the case between Leza and Sewa, the problem was that when Sewa needed him most he was unavailable.

He was at war, but Sewa didn't know that, the night before he left he had promised himself to her as her husband, promising her that he would always protect her and keep her happy.

You should know that the southafrican pantheon gods take promises seriously, they take them as vows.

So when the invaders killed all of Sewa's family and friends while she was away at a crossroad waiting for leza, she bacame distraught. "I feel myself getting involved in the story and I lean closer, she continues.

" She wanted to ask the gods why? Hadn't she paid her dues? When worshipped them, even, she was promised to one of them, so in her grief she started climbing to the sky, took her weaving basket and weaved all day and night, weaved so she could get to her Leza.

But the gods being the jealous beings that they are could not abide that a human, a measly human was gaining on them, was almost at there door mat, so they pushed her back to earth.

She fell but survived, she survived and waited for Leza, waited all day and night, summer passed, winter too and still no Leza, eventually she died of her grief.

Leza, unknown to him was still at war, fighting to protect his people, when he got back he saw that the invaders had gotten to his people he was distraught, almost ran mad when he saw that his Sewa was no more.

He actually ran mad for 2 years and eventually he was called back to come resume his duty.

When he got back, things were not as he thought it would be, he wanted to lock himself away and lick his wounds but mujaji, the mother of rainfall and all women had another thing for him.

Seeing as mujaji was the mother of women she was really angered when Sewa died, so he brought leza to the presence of the other gods, she made him own up to the promise that he made, the promise that he would always protect his woman.

Leza being distraught and guilty with grief did nothing to defend himself so he was saddled with a job.

To always protect women of the bantu tribe, no matter when they call on him, no matter the danger to him self.

So if any south African woman who believes enough makes a wish to be protected she would, no matter what, it's a curse and a blessing, you have to be a devoted worshipper and you just have to believe, I am a devoted worshipper so I am always protected by Leza"

Mimi scoffs even as I feel my self facinated at the concept.

"You really believe in that bull? C

Mimi asks and Honey throws her a weird smile that I find disturbing." Trust me Mimi, very soon you will be made a believer "

She says and I thank her.

"Thank you for the story Honey, I feel a little better "

She nods and my mind wanders to the story, how much grief Leza must have felt when he lost his woman.

I send a silent prayer above.

Even if I am not south African and I am not under your protection I know what I you must have gone through, I am sorry about that, no one should ever go through that, even a god.

But please, protect me and my family, we are human too"

I send the prayer above and the weirdest thing happens.

I feel a warm breeze blow my neck and my migraine abates.

I close my eyes for a second and when I open my eyes I see Honey looking at me in an intense way.I throw her a look and she looks away.

*****Leza listens to the heartfelt prayer and he smiles.

The woman is pure, the woman sounded just like his Sewa, just like his love.

He looked closely again and he smiles, sending his healing wind from the west to her.

He understood now, he didn't make a mistake keeping her alive.

AN.

Is it just me or was that intense?Tell me what you think.

Don't forget to do the thing, yup the thing.

Much love, muah.

Chapter Thirty Three

G arrett.

I see Will lift his eyebrows with playful glee and I know, I just know something was wrong with him upstairs.

"You really think you can bet your of this alive?"

"I think you are going to let me get out of this alive?"

"Pray tell why would I do such a fool thing??"

"Because William, I know you, I know how you crave to be a good guy, I know how you are a person pleaser, don't you want to serve your Master?"

I say referring to me and I see him twitch, that's right, I hit the nail on the head, Will must be doing this for some one else or for his selfish reasons.

The Will I thought I knew would have been distraught to go against me, only God knows why he is on this now.

"Are you on drugs?? I am the one with the gun here, I am the master here"He says and I feel Marcel shuffle on a feet behind me.

I signal to him behind my back with my hands and I pray to God that he understands.

"Don't you see how helpless you are? You and your idiot brother, you thought you had it all, you had a woman, you have a child.

I want those things too, I saw her first you know, Kismet, I saw her first in that airport, I wanted to approach but you had to be a diva and cry about the plane not being fueled, then you had her and I had to watch you make family with her, listened to her cry out a thousand time from behind your bedroom door, broke me"

And there it is, the key behind everything.

"She is my woman Will"

"She is my woman Garrett"

"What then? You think I if you kill me she will automatically love you? Automatically want you? You are a fool Will"

He growls softly at my words and I feel pure fucking thrill run through me, this fucker had stood outside the door to my bedroom when I and my woman did things, private things, things that were beautiful and should never be shared with an outsider, things that I cherished with my bones and things that were so beautiful they created my child.

This fucker is going to die, no qualms about it.

"You should be wise and shut up Garrett fucking Grayson!!""Why is that Will fucking Iam?"

"Because I have a gun! A gun!""Well William, you have a gun, I have a big shiny gun"

I say as I whip out the gun Marcel had delivered into my hands, my brother wasn't so useless after all.

I pop Marcel one on the knees and.he cries out, his gun falling and skittering away from him.

I knee beside him when he begins to bleed and groan.

"You see Will, I take care of my family and I also take care of the people who betray me, you must know that I never hold a grudge but when I do, I never fucking let it go"

I say to him and he groans again, giving me a dead look.

"Well, good day, you can tell the Shaws that they can find another killing machine"..

I say before popping him another one in his other knee, he cries out again, blood flows and stains the ground by him and I don't even feel a single fucking thing.

I stand to step away when his blood leaks to my boot I begin to walk away but I turn.

" And William, do not think to cross me ever again, the next time, you won't be leaving with your life"

I say before walking out and I feel Marcel walking behind me.

"You know he would be back, you know, why didn't you just finish him"

"I want to give him him the benefit of the doubt, in respect to his years of service"

"That's bull Gage and you know it"I throw Marcel a smile that was pure teeth as I open my car.

"You know me too well, brada"I say before getting in.

Marcel will be back, with an army and I can tell, don't you think it is fitting that I know who my enemies are?

Hell.

AN.

Hola Hola,Whatcha doing today.

It's asks Bebe anything you want Friday,Ask me any questions about me and I will try to answer as truthfully as I can.

Any question at all.

And as you know I am ending beautiful mess soon, thanks for being along for the ride.

My sincerest apologies if at any time I didn't reply your comments, I was really busy during the writing of this novel, I wrote on the go and I appreciate that you could understand.

I love you.

I promise to deliver another package soon and I hope you enjoy it.

and also please, DO NOT READ MY NOVEL AND COPY IT WITH-OUT MY PERMISSION, It hurts when you do.

I had thoughts of even stopping beautiful Mess half way because I was beyond depressed but ya'll kept me standing tall and going.

Thanks for reading and always being here, amazes me that I have people like you behind me, cheering me on.

So please ask me anything about me and the book or any future books and covers, I will answer.

And also, Facebook fams, ya'll ain't left out, please ask.

Kadosh, where are you at?.?You done reading in whispers?

Much love sweetness.

Chapter Thirty Four

Beautiful Mess   Jason Mraz

Garrett.

The tremblings woke me up, i roll over from where I turned away from Kismet and I see her.

She's the source of the trembling.

"Kis?"

"Garr? Something's wrong"

"Stay with me baby, I'm going to get an ambulance"

"OK..."

She say with a weak voice and I roll over out of the bed to pull on my pajamas trousers.

I slip on the jacket and I don't get to button it before she begins to buck.I feel fear course through me as I hit the bed lifting her up.

"Garrett, I don't feel so good""I'm right here angel"

I pick her up and I grab my car keys and exit my room.

I see Mimi and honey sitting at the table, they must have being on there way to bed because they look startled.

I and Kismet had an early evening in and we went to bed early.

I am thinking that was a wrong move.

"What's wrong??"

"Get an ambulance, Kismet is not fine.."

"What...""Now Mimi!!!"

She responds quickly and dials the emergency number,.

"Garrett??...""Stay with me Hazel eyes"

I say.

"It's happening"

Honey days in an ominous voice and I turn to her, knowing, just knowing that I cant kill her no matter what.

I hear sirens and I turn to Mimi."I will stay with Kismet, get a car and bring jazz"

I say and she gives a short nod.

****

"I don't think she is gonna make it this time sir"

I listen to the doctor shatter my world and I take a step back.

"What do you mean this time?"

"I don't know if she told you but I was the doctor that helped her in her delivery, she died then but came back to life.

Now it seems as if her body is shutting down"I almost tell the doctor that no, no infact she didn't tell me about him but I don't as I try to digest this new piece of information.

She died?My Kismet died?

Now she isn't going to make it?

I falter as my eyes go to the bed where she seems to have aged a thousand years.

I turn to the doctor.

"Do something"

I say.

"I'm sorry sir, we haven't seen anything like this, she is wasting away too fast and we can't do anything"

"My wife is not wasting away,! She isn't!"

"Please calm down sir."

"FUCKING FUCK!!!!!"

I scream as my hand grabs chunk of my hair to pull.

The door opens and Mimi steps in, tears in her eyes, jazz is standing beside her.

They heard everything.

"Daddy??"

"Come here doll" She falls into my arms.

"Do something daddy"

I close my eyes as helplessness washes over me and I know, I know what I have to do.

"Mimi, where's honey?"

"She's in the waiting room"

"Stay here with jasmin, I will be out a while"

I say and she nods and I see the fear in her eyes and I feel that helplessness run through me again.

I walk to the waiting room.

"I was waiting for you" She says when I step in and I nod.

"You know what's wrong" I say not as a question but a statement and she nods.

"Fix it" I say and she shakes her head again.

"You have to fix it honey, you have to fucking give me back my life"

"I'm sorry it's beyond my control, I'm sorry this is happening to Kismet but it has to happen, you brought it on your self"

I fall to my knees as I beg for my wife's life.

"Please, fix it"

I say again and this time she doesn't respond, the door to the waiting room opens and a man walks in.

At first I turned from him but at another glance he holds my attention.

I turn to honey to see her head bowed at the man and I turn back to him.

"Garrett Grayson" He says and in his voice I hear a thousand voices.

"I seriously don't do this, but I just had to come"

He says and his voice reminds of the voice in my head.

"You are getting what you deserve but I am a benevolent God and I give what I can of myself"

He says and I lift my eyes.

"Who are you?" I finally asks.

"I am the god who saved your wife's life when you really asked for it, I am the God who protects my own, I am Leza"

He says and I believe him.

"Why are you doing this?"

I ask and he shakes his head.

"You did this, you did this all by yourself Garrett Grayson"

"What?"

"You came into my land and asked for my help, I gave it, not considering that you were there to kill my people, you Garrett Grayson are a very brave but selfish man.

You felt your soul mate dying and you asked for my help but at the time the blood of my people were staining your hands "

As he says this images flies through my head and I remember, remember asking for help to any God who could hear me to please protect my Kismet.

" I protected your woman Garrett Grayson, I gave her your life and now the life is crying to belong to one person, you must decide if you want her to die or you want to die, this is your punishment for killing my people"

He says and there is no doubt to my answer.As I answer my life flashes before my eyes .

"Please, take my life"

I say and he nods.

"So Be It"He says and I feel instantly as the life drains from me.

As I feel my self weaken I send a silent prayer to the heaven and I see Leza, the god, smile.

Please, most high, in my next life, bless me with more luck.

I think this as as I close my eyes.

Kismet.

I open my eyes to know that something was definitely wrong.

"You are awake!!"

Mimi shouts and I turn to her.

"Where is Garrett?""He just went out to get...."

I cry out when I feel the pain in my chest and my hand clutches my chest.

I bring my hands away form my chest and I see it coated with blood.

And I know, I just know that my Garrett is dead.

AN.Heya, hope you enjoyed beautiful Mess.

Thanks for all the comments and votes

Thanks for coming along for the ride, thank you sweetness.

Chapter Thirty Five

BeautifulCrush

Kismet.

5 years later.

"I wish daddy was here"Jasmin says as we stand in front of the boarding school.I feel that familiar longing course through me and I squeeze her hands.

"It's fine baby girl"I say as I kiss her head.

My baby is a grown girl now, she is even going to boarding school and everything.

"I will miss you Maman" she says and I nod, not trying to say anything so I won't cry.

Coupled with my longing for Garrett and other things I will totally break.

I watch as she drags her suitcases in and I wave goodbye.

She disappears out of site and I wipe my tears before getting into the car.

I drive the long distance home and it takes me two hours.

When I get home I slide the double door of the beach house open and our dog, bates runs out.

"Hello, boy, did you miss me?"I ask and he gives a woof.

I smile at him and I walk in.I got Bates when the loneliness got too much.

It was too lonely at night.I make some coffee, I begin to take a dip when the double doors slide open.

"Is she gone yet?"Garrett asks in an expectant tone and I squeal.

"You are home?!"

"I told you I would be back, why are you so surprised?"

He asks and I pepper his face with kisses.

"I know you said that but you know I can't be far from you, you were gone for two weeks"

I say and he kisses my lips deeply before swinging me around."I'm sorry"He says and he sets me down.

I nod before answering his earlier question."Yes, she is at the boarding school already, she missed you, will you go see her next week?"

"I will"He says as he bends down to scratch Bates who has been trying to get his attention.

"Do you want to go see her?"He asks and I nod, the familiar pain going through me as I remember.

We walk towards the back of the house and get onto the bike there.

He drives us down to the cemetery and we get off.

We walk hand in hand down to the grave as I bend to pick sunflowers to place at her grave.

I sit by it and I begin to speak.

"Hey Mimi, how are you?"

As usual there is no response, I feel Garrett get down beside me and I lean into him.

"Hey brat, how have you been? I am back from my trip"

Garrett says and I hit his hand at the brat comment.

He laughs and we sit a while watching the sun and the clouds.

When I felt like I had lost my husband a man had stepped in, he had given me a choice, telling me I could choose between my self and Garrett.

Mimi paid the ultimate price, giving her life for Garrett's.

At the time I did not know what it meant but I later found out that Mimi was never coming back.

After that Garrett told me everything, everything about himself, how he was supposed to kill the Osei family and how Honey also know as Stephanie was the last he was supposed to kill.

About Will's betrayal, how Will wanted me and wanted to be like Garrett and how Will almost killed him.

The bastard.

Marcel comes to visit once a while and it's good to have a family of Garrett's.

His mom is still not interested in us so we are also waiting for her to come around.

We haven't heard anything from the Shaws and William and I hope that is the last of it.

"What are you thinking about?"

He whispers in my ear and I smile.

"How lucky we are to have a god watching over us"

I say and he kisses my neck.

"We aren't lucky baby girl, we deserve it and everything"

I nod because I know it's true. I turn around to kiss his head.

"I love you Kis"

He says and I nod.

"Love you too, Garrett"

We stay like that and I feel full to bursting, I feel happy.

Yeah, it was good, my Beautiful Mess was and is still worth it.

The End

www.ingramcontent.com/pod-product-compliance
Lightning Source LLC
Chambersburg PA
CBHW070312190726
48291CB00012B/1083